LOOSE ENDS

LOOSE ENDS

J O H N   A N D E S

iUniverse LLC
Bloomington

LOOSE ENDS

iUniverse books may be ordered through booksellers or by contacting:

iUniverse LLC
1663 Liberty Drive
Bloomington, IN 47403
www.iuniverse.com
1-800-Authors (1-800-288-4677)

ISBN: 978-1-4917-0551-3 (sc)
ISBN: 978-1-4917-0582-7 (ebk)

Printed in the United States of America

iUniverse rev. date: 08/21/2013

Plan your work and work your plan.
The better your plan, the better your work,
unless people are involved.

Saturday Night
and Sunday Morning

1:25 AM. Where is she? She said she was going to stop and have a drink with some friends after her shift. Her shift ended over three hours ago. Where is she? Is she up to her old tricks? Has she met some guy, who buys her drinks, tells how beautiful she is and how she's wasting her time with a boring shopkeeper; an older guy like me? Has she just decided to get falling down drunk to express her anger at me for some unknown grievance? Is she angry with me or her own failures in life? Will she come home or go with him? Or will she be helped to the couch in the den of one her nursing pals? Drunk or stoned on stolen meds. The knot in my stomach is dull yet all-inclusive. I had this feeling years ago when my young wife decided to search for a lover. I nod off.

I am awakened by the premonition that something evil or wrong is happening. I am awakened by the feeling of dread. Of abandonment. My eyes open and will not close. I get out of bed, take a pee, get a drink of water, and struggle to get back to sleep. The greater the struggle, the greater the odds of not sleeping. Late night cable TV is a distraction, but it is not sleep inducing. I pace. I worry. I feel sorry for myself. This is an old set of circumstances and feelings. It goes back to when I was a child and my mother was institutionalized . . . depression fueled by prescription medicines and booze. She was found sitting on the attic windowsill in her nightgown. Dad and his brother, the doctor, got her to an institution for rest, therapy and a regimen of strong medication.

She stayed there for a year. I waited for her to come back to me. I thought it was all my fault. Maybe it was. Maybe I was just too much of a hassle, a burden for her. A year after she came home she had another child. Now I was not the baby. Once again I was abandoned. These two events set the pattern of my relationships with women. Meet and charm them. Love them and be loved. Push the relationship. Demand control. Exhibit infantile jealousy. Push them away in fits of irrationality. Feel abandonment deeply. Make it happen. Complete the process. Experience the self-fulfilling prophecy of my perceived relationship with my mother. Be alone and lonely. Only to repeat the cycle with other women who love me. Maybe if Ellie and I were married, she would take our relationship more seriously. Maybe she would love me enough not to hurt me. Maybe I could explain all this to her, if we were married.

Why am I even here at all? Dad wanted me to get an Ivy League education and Brown wanted a point guard; a floor general. The marriage was set. We won the Ivy League Championship my senior year. Then the wheels fell off. That spring, Mom died in a auto accident, and Dad fell into a deep depression. He begged me to come home and run the family business; The *Bric's Hardware Store*. My sister, the selfish bitch, had built her own life in Montana, and was not about to give that up. I was the only one left. I yielded to paternal pleas, and took over the store. Within one year Dad died. I suspect of a broken heart. But I know alcohol fueled his demise. So, here I am. Stuck in nowhere Minnesota. The economy is crumbling, and the hope of getting out of the mess is slim, very slim. My dreams of world domination have been reduced to kegs of nails, racks of tools, and stacks of late notices, both the companies and our customers. My present situation is proof that no good deed goes unpunished.

Every noise gets my attention. The ensuing silence fuels my anxiety. No slam of a car door. No turn of the front door handle. The headlights of a car passing my driveway spike my hope that she has come back to me. The darkness that follows mirrors my gloom. The myriad minutiae that bounce through my brain have become large jagged thoughts painfully scraping my soul. I think about what I have to do tomorrow ... or today. File the last report. Pick up dry cleaning. Get gas. Call about the past due accounts. Each task ends with her. Or with her and me. Only now there is no her. Only me. I have to be better so she will be there. What does she want me to do to prove my devotion?

The usual fare of soft porn and grade B action movies. Thank God Ted Turner shows classic films twenty-four/seven. Black and white cops and robbers grist. Musicals that got our minds off the Cold War and the Red Menace. I need a drink. And a joint. Scotch neat and good grass will ease me back to the land of nod. So I pour and roll. Fire up the stick. Sip the warmth. The edges soften. The points of pain are numbed. Light from the TV fills the room as if all the floor and ceiling lights were on. The room changes shape and composition as the scenes of the movie change. It's almost as if the furniture is being moved. Frank Lovejoy, Aldo Ray and some studio starlet in training are arguing at a kitchen table. A car pulls into the drive and up to the door. Its lights shine through the four windowpanes and filmy curtain on the back door. They react with dread. They are silent. Lovejoy reaches for the light switch. Ray and the girl stand flat against the wall trying to be invisible. The car door closes. The camera moves into to the doorknob as it turns. The door is opened and the camera pans up to the intruder. It's Ellie. Home at last

"Have you been waiting up for me, Bric? How sweet. Sorry, I'm so late. But, my relief was late. She had car trouble. Then I really needed a drink. By the time I got to Billy's, everybody was leaving. They stayed for my drink and bought me a second. But, I'm home now. Tired. I need a shower. And I could use some of what you are smoking. It was a mother of a shift. Two auto accidents. Twelve people all banged up. And Mr. Swanson, you know the old man, who runs the smoke and gift shop at the mall. Well, he slipped on the ice in the parking lot and fractured his hip and two ribs. Tonight the ER was so damned crowded with patients, doctors, staff, families and lawyers; I just wanted to disappear into the sunshine ... on the beach, sipping fruity drinks, and covering our bodies with oil. I'll take a few hits now."

After the stick was gone and she had showered, Ellie came to bed. I was almost asleep when she aroused me. I took her with feral ferocity. She was there for me with full blow passionate dispassion. Sunlight seared my eyes. I was late.

* *

Being late makes the drive to work easier, because there is less traffic. Today my goal was to work on the ever growing past due folder. Make the threatening calls. Then, send someone to the customer to collect the agreed-to payment. Cash. No bad checks. We have enough of them already. For the really big problems . . . the ones who owe the store over seven grand, I should go myself. A little face time never hurt. It showed that we were not trying to strong-arm the debtor, just get what was legally ours. And, I could hint that we still wanted them as a customer. Today I am the *Cunning Collector*.

The *Bric's Hardware Store* provides an alomost decent living for eight families. I had to resurrect the business by pumping a lot of sweat and borrowed money into it after dad drank the cash register dry. Beyond me, there are clerks and drivers. We all do multiple jobs to keep the personnel to the minimum and pay to the maximum. No turnover in three years. Everybody seems happy with their lots. But, keeping the downtown business going in the face of the chain stores, anchors at the two malls, is becoming increasingly difficult. That's why collections had to be handled with a smile and kind words of promise. We would continue to extend credit if regular payments were made. But, we're really between a rock and a hard place.

Too much money is tied up in inventory. Money we could recoup if our customers paid for what they bought. We had been behind the curve by extending credit in the glimmer of an economic uptick. No such luck. Now the subcontractors, who were always betting on the next job, are shit out of luck, because there are fewer and fewer and smaller and smaller "next jobs". Plus, they spent their draws, and not on supplies. On their own mortgages and car payments. So, The *Bric's Hardware Store* was left holding the bag filled with promises to pay, while we had to pay just to keep our shelves stocked. We must do everything possible to avoid empty shelves. Empty shelves are sure signs of retail death.

* *

"Jonteil, have you run a tab on our past dues?"

"It's in the folder three ways, alphabetized, ranked by amount, and ranked by age."

"Thanks. Goddamn it, $156,548. Are you sure we're that deep? Have we paid the sales tax on all this?"

"No. Just the ones that are over ninety days. That keeps the state from being nosey. I got a call from Ben Gustafson in Minneapolis yesterday. He's reminded me that we haven't paid Midwest Distribution anything for over ninety days."

"Don't worry about Ben. I'll take care of Midwest. Your assignment, if you choose to accept it, is to join me in an aggressive program of collection. For the next two days, with everything else you and I do, we will call these beloved deadbeats and browbeat them into paying all or a large portion of their bill. We will settle for nothing less than a single payment that covers our cost of the goods sold and the taxes owed. The balance, our mark up and taxes, will be due and payable in two installments over the next sixty days. We will drive to our clients and retrieve cash, or we will accept their credit card information over the phone. Either way, we will be paid. I'll call the customers on this list. You can call the others. By the way, you can be as forceful as you need to be to get the money. Remember, it's your money, too."

* *

With all the television bravado of the Impossible Mission Force, we set upon two days of unfriendly persuasion. Dialing and smiling. Setting appointments. Returning empty handed, because the target was "away from the job". After, two of these non-events, we plan to ambush the noncompliant payee wannabes at their homes after work. A little familial embarrassment might facilitate fiduciary responsibility. Hopefully it will work.

Jonteil got cash from the cookie can under the sink. I got fifteen crisp one hundred dollar bills, apparently being saved for a rainy day. It rained that night. The net of all our cajoling and coercion was that we collected on less than a ten percent of the total number of outstanding invoices, just three of the receivables, which were 90 days or older, and none of the forty really big ones. I gave Jonteil thirty dollars for the use of her car. Next week we'll repeat this process. Our quarter ends in three weeks. We have to be liquid by then. Or, we will have to plan our own funeral.

* *

Saturday. Fishing with Tommy and Marilee Bowen. The four of us fish every other weekend throughout the year. More of an outing. Most times we don't catch anything worth keeping. The boat, picnic basket, and lots of beer. By the end of the day, who cares or knows if we've caught anything. Dinner at *Nooners*. Meat and scotch. Dancing and laughter.

"Tommy, I heard they're going to start layoffs soon at the plant. Is that true?"

"I can't say."

"You can't say or won't say?"

"I know, but can't say."

"Jesusfuckingchrist. What this town does not need now is layoffs at the plant. I mean, there are about twelve hundred families that rely on the plant for their mortgage, bread and butter. If layoffs start, many good people will be on the street. And the ripple effect will be terrible. Groceries won't get bought. Loans won't be repaid. Money, earmarked for jobs around he house or a new car, will be used for essentials. As the plant goes, so goes the town. So go all the merchants. So go I. How many people will be let go?"

"Between the four of us, management has decided to start with 120. If that 10% cut works to get the books in balance with production, they will stop. If not, more layoffs will be needed. Maybe another batch in four or five months. Until the finances are made true. They discussed across the board wage cuts to hold jobs, but the union balked. I think the union wants to get rid of some troublemakers. The layoffs will be at all levels. Seniority might protect some. So substitutes will have to be found."

"You know what we need to do? We need to fold our tents and get out of town before it folds in on us."

"Jesus, Bric, you're sounding paranoid. We should stick it out. We can weather this storm, just like a Saskatchewan Screamer. Hunker in the bunker."

"Marilee, I'm scared, but not crazy. I just spent two days trying to collect past due bills. Jonteil and I only scratched the surface. It was hardly worth the effort if you consider the bad will the effort generated and the value of our hours. The people aren't paying now because they spent money that wasn't theirs to spend and no replacement money has come in. They fucked up and we fucked up because we extended them credit. They have no money to pay us and we can't pay our wholesalers. The banks won't lend us money on our receivables, because the people who are the receivables already owe the bank more than they can pay. They won't lend us money on our inventory, because it's not ours . . . we haven't paid for it.

The wholesalers will decide soon to come and repossess what is theirs. Our shelves will be as empty as our bank account. The stench of death will fill the store and we will close. If you don't think a crisis is coming, Marilee, tomorrow check out the school and the school district. See if there are spending slow downs or deferrals. Maybe outright elimination of budgeted items. Administration jobs that are going to be consolidated."

"Bric, you're being melodramatic. Things can't be that bad."

"For us at the store, they are that bad. Maybe not now for the rest of you, but they'll get that way real soon. I had been guessing 30-45 days before the newspaper starts to write about the impending economic death. The City Council will put pressure on the paper to sit on the story to avoid a city wide panic. But, with the plant layoffs, the death knell will sound in a few weeks. Shit, unemployment is already in the low teens. The plant layoffs and the first collateral ripples will push it to twenty. The only way we can avoid the mess is to take a strong, positive step now. Move on. Start fresh somewhere else."

"Why don't we just rob the bank?"

"Tommy, that's not as dumb as you might think."

"Bric, I was kidding. Now you're being an asshole."

"Would we be able to visit you guys and your new best friends on Sundays? We'll bring pies and cigarettes you can trade for sex."

"Marilee, think long and hard about your financial future, before you shit all over my worries."

"This conversation is getting too deep and too dark for me. It's late. The day has been long. Let's finish up and go home."

The ride home is deadly silent.

* *

"Ellie, what are you pissed about, now?"

"I'm not pissed, Bric. I'm scared. Scared of your fear. Scared of the depth of your fear. And scared that you might be right. I don't want to leave town. Duluth is the only place I've ever lived. And, I don't want to do something really stupid or really illegal. I think we can stay here and work through this mess."

"You're either blind or more naïve than I thought. The economy is circling the porcelain bowl. You don't see it because Saint Mary's Hospital is sheltered from the impending crash. The hospital is funded by the state. The state is bound to provide health care funded by taxes. They may stop road, or prison, or education projects for a while, but the men in St. Paul will never stop paying for health care.

It's their job security. It gets them elected and re-elected. Hell, it's your job security. I'm in the free market and fewer people are buying what I'm selling. And, those who bought last month are not paying. It's going to get worse before it gets better. I just want to avoid being swept away with the rest of the failed small business owners. You can help or not."

"I'll help anyway I can, you know that. It's just that I don't see the danger right now."

"It may not be here now. But, it will be here very soon. Next month at the latest. I just want us to be ahead of it. OK?"

"OK."

* *

Sunday is three-on-three hoops at the Y. Tommy, Omar, and I are Team K in the league. Omar Williams is Jonteil's husband. He is an engineer for the county, who can't dunk and is no deep threat. An anomaly for a black man. But, he handles the ball like it's an extension of his hands and his D is ferocious. We won the league last year, and figure to this year, except two other squads are built around recent graduates from East High's team that went to the state semis. Today we have two easy games. Shower and off to the hotel for their buffet brunch.

* *

"Bric, you're ranting really scared Marilee last night. And, I don't mind telling you I thought some of the stuff was extreme."

"Whoa, fill me in on what was said."

"Bric was foretelling economic doom and gloom. And how we could avoid being crushed in the avalanche."

"Jonteil, told me about your dialin', smilin', trippin' and clippin' routine this past week. Said it wasn't all that fruitful. Are things getting that tight at the store?"

"We are beginning to be squeezed by no payments on one side and demands for payment or return of merchandise on the other. Merchandise, which, by the way, we no longer have, because the guys who can't pay us have already used it. This is the first step in the process of failure. I am trying my damnedest to stop the process. Then I heard about the pending layoffs at the plant and I could picture the ripple effect on my business. Tommy confirmed it last night. I am more than just wary, I'm scared."

"Plant layoffs? What's that all about, Tommy?"

"The rumors are that there will be some layoffs."

"Rumors? Some? Give me a damned break. You know more than you're telling."

"Omar, here's the deal. If I tell you and you talk, I'll have to kill you."

"Tommy, if you don't tell me you'll never see another pass as long as we play in the league."

"Take my first born, but don't threaten me with that. I'll talk. I'll talk. Management has decided that to bring the books in line, they need to "rightsize" by a specific dollar amount, and that represents about 120 people. Interestingly none of those to be cut are upper management. The big salaried guys. If this step is successful, the employees will be rehired when the economy turns around."

"What if the sacrifice of 120 is not successful?"

"Then the process will be repeated, until the income exceeds the outgo and the plant is in a positive cash mode."

"Omar, can you see what will happen once this step is taken. Not only will the town lose the spending of the 120 families; it will see a cut back among those who fear for their jobs. The retail sector will suffer right after the layoffs. Hell, your part of the government will probably have to cut back, because there will be less tax revenue."

"That explains a lot."

"Like what?"

"Last month I was due for a performance review, which customarily means a cost-of-living increase every six months. Despite my repeated questions, my boss does not want to talk about my reveiw. On top of that, about six weeks ago, a hiring freeze was put in effect. We thought we needed at least three more people to handle the road, environmental, and school projects that were in the pipeline. All the planning for the future work was put on hold, too. Plus, the rumor around the buildings is that there will be no bonuses this year. The darkest whisper is that we may even have to reduce our staff of non-essential personnel, whoever the hell they are."

"See, Tommy, it's already started. The government forecasters have known for some time. They are just bureaucratically slow to act. It's deeper and broader than we thought."

"Bric, that's than *you* thought."

"So, what's this about leaving town?"

"Look, leaving town and starting fresh is not as harebrained as Tommy might think. We all have marketable skills. We not encumbered by children. We could just pack-up and leave."

"A little desperate, but doable."

"Tommy's conversation last night deteriorated to bank robbery."

"Robbing a bank is very desperate, very dumb, and very illegal."

"Look, I'll level with you guys. I haven't pulled a salary from the store in eight months. I loan myself just enough to pay my bills . . . mortgage, car note and this boat. I'm going to get clobbered at tax time. Ellie's income pays for everything else. I borrowed up to the max at the bank when I bought out my partners and corrected Dad's shortcomings. I'm on the cuff to the wholesalers for more than I ever thought possible. If, the store doesn't get well very soon, I'm going to have to shutter the doors. Omar, that means Jonteil will be out of work in a town where 120 other people are about to be dumped on the street. Not a promising situation. Who want's another Bloody Mary?"

The rest of the post-game banquet was spent in silence under the specter of financial destruction. We decided to go to the boat to discuss the situation without listeners, and with appropriate mind expansion.

* *

"Rob a bank. Y'all must be crazy."

After a few hits, Omar slipped away from his seven years of expensive Ivy League education into the tone and lexicon of the street. It was all an act. His parents were doctors in Chicago, and his sister was a Biochemist working for ADM.

"This brother be no Jesse James or Dillinger. He be just an engineer working for the gummit."

"Well, bro, the gummit may not want you working for it very soon. Just think about your lot in life. You're a well-paid well-educated black man who is doing the job an undereducated white guy would love to do. The politicians rely on a white constituency. And this is a white bread, mayonnaise, and whole milk part of the world. Strange reversal of affirmative action, eh what? How many other black families or couples live within twenty miles? Two? Five? Ten?

And what kind of jobs do they have? Garbage hauler? Handyman? Railroad worker? It's very simple; this part of the world is not openly hospitable to people of color . . . blacks, Hispanics, or indigenous Indians. So, politicians, and that's who runs your business, would have no qualms about dumping your black butt on the street and replacing you with a very loyal white cousin. Think about your future."

"We're not criminals."

"No, we're three guys, who see the writing on the wall and don't like the message. I don't like the concept of sneaking away under the cover of darkness and becoming a clerk in some *Bric's Hardware Store* in Denver or Phoenix. If I'm going to leave, it's going to be for safety and a better life. That requires more money than I have."

"There aren't many food manufacturing plant jobs calling my name. Jobs that offer a similar salary and little or no stress. Frankly, the more I think of the layoffs, the more I fear the second round. I mean, I don't have nearly the seniority of a lot of guys under me. Guys, who could do my job in a pinch. And this is a pinch. So, I figure, I will be in the next group that gets handed little pink slips."

"What kind of severance are they giving the soon to be departed?"

"Two weeks plus unused vacation time. For me, that would amount to a grand total of four weeks. Maybe a little more, but I doubt it. Certainly, no retirement nest egg. If I get the axe, I'd have to leave town. I seriously doubt if the plant will be in a rehiring mode for about a year or eighteen months at the earliest. That's just too long to hold out on the promise of a maybe. So, I'm fucked. Therefore, I'd rather leave under my own initiative. Maybe, Marilee and I should just pack up and move somewhere to start over. I don't know, but it looks better every time I look at the alternative."

"How are we going to do all this resettlement without cash? Jonteil and I have some money, but not enough to move somewhere and start fresh without a job."

"The way I see it, we need enough cash to carry us out of the country or at the very least provide anonymous safety in the US for two years or so. Until we can emerge from under the rocks and into the sunshine. That's more cash than I have without stealing from a bank."

"Bric, what the hell would happen to the store?"

"Just leave it to the bank and suppliers."

"How much cash do you think *Shaft, Butch,* and *Sundance* need?"

"I figure we need about 100 grand each. That should keep us going for two years. Longer if we can land simple jobs in our new 'hoods."

"Where the hell are we going to lay our hands on 300 grand?"

"That's part of the plan we need to work on. The problem is personal economic destruction. The issue is survival. The timing is now. The solution is money. The amount is 300 grand. Attendant to an amount of this size is departure from the area of acquisition. All I ask is that you guys think about my proposition. And all of this remains between us . . . no wives or sweeties are to be involved."

Monday, Monday

"Bric, it's for you on line 3."

"Hello, this is Bric, how may I help you?"

"Bric, it's me, Tommy. I just got the really bad news. I'm on the list of expendables. It seems that some old fart with five more years than I've got, convinced somebody he could do my job. And they agreed. Given the fact that he probably makes eight grand a year less than I do, management is getting a bargain. An inept bargain, but a bargain nonetheless. I'm fucked. How the hell am I going to explain this to Marilee."

"Slow down, Tommy. How did you learn all this?"

"Gus, the guy who knew my dad, called me in for coffee and told me I should be looking to protect myself. Told me to make sure I knew the precise value of my benefits . . . vacation days, pension plan, health insurance, and life insurance . . . because I would need to know this information. When I asked what the hell he meant, he told me flat out that management and the union did some 6H-pencil work over the weekend. They figured out they could layoff a fewer guys if they dumped managers and replaced us with stalwart union toadies from the floor.

For the two camps it's a win-win situation. The two sides are in bed together, but the managers got screwed. Tried and true union guys keep their jobs. Some get promoted. Then they owe even more loyalty to the union. The union comes out a winner as it digs into my level of management. The promoted guys will lose overtime earnings, but they will be replacing guys like me who made more than they did to begin with. Their raise will be about half the difference between their over time money and the salary level they are promoted to. And that won't happen for six months. Enough time for the company to solve its financial problems. The company saves money at both ends, and looks like it appreciates the union. All twenty-four managers are getting dumped. Bric, what the hell am I going to do now."

"Do what Gus says. It would not surprise me if the company offers a package, which is less than you compute. They'll probably try to short your health insurance coverage by three months and cut your life insurance policy immediately. You might be able to bargain these two points. They won't make any contribution to your pension fund after this week. Maybe they haven't made a contribution for a while with the excuse that they were going to make a big contribution at the end of the year. When was the last statement you got? Tommy, you've got to protect yourself."

"I can get all the up-to-date information together in two days. When I contact our benefits people, they'll know that I know. Won't that trigger an alarm?"

"Tommy, if Gus is right, an alarm is the last thing you need to worry about. In fact an alarm may work to your advantage. If they know that you know, they won't have an advantage of surprise. You'll have all the facts. And, if your facts differ from their facts, you will be in control. If they're lying to you, you can get a better deal. You can advise them that you know the truth and you'd like to discuss it with the State Labor Board. The last thing the company and the union want is for the manager mass execution and the promotion of the unskilled to be examined by the State Labor Board.

The company can deal with an investigation into the lay off of hourly wage earners. It happens all the time. That's why there are union funds, unemployment insurance, and state funded health insurance. The union will back the company because the union and company are working together. But, the company and union will want all of the managers to go quietly into the night, because the wholesale dismissal and replacement action is not easily defended. So, a way for you to gain the upper hand in any settlement is to make it negotiated. Don't take what they offer; they have more than they want to put on the table."

"Sounds good, Bric. And, you know our discussion yesterday? That sounds even better. They key will be . . . how did you put it . . . acquisition. I think I'll work on that as my next career project. I certainly don't have to put much thought into this place much longer."

"Tommy don't do something stupid, and don't tell Marilee anything until you learn it officially. Did Gus say when all this was going to happen?"

"Friday."

"Hang tough Tommy. Call me if you learn anything more, or if you just want to talk."

* *

Click. The bomb is about to drop. This week's calling and collecting has to start now. Before the shock waves cause even greater financial damage to retail business. Time is of the essence.

"Jonteil, let's pick up where we left off last Friday. Go back to our lists and re-contact everybody. This time we'll tell them that if they make no attempt to settle their account, we are prepared to notify all other merchants, the Chamber of Commerce, and the Better Business Bureau that the customer is a deadbeat. And, we'll make the notification the day after tomorrow."

"Bric, it's not in my place, but don't you think that's a little harsh?"

"Protecting the jobs of my employees and the life of my store requires hard decisions and strong actions. Jonteil, jobs are at risk. The store is in imminent danger. We are not yet at the point of do or die, and I don't want to be there. So, it's time for you and I to take strong actions. As with last week, we will drive to the customer's home or place of business to collect cash. Now, drop whatever you thought you were going to do today and get crackin'."

The first two on my list did not take kindly to threats. I explained my words were not meant to threaten. They were meant to explain the gravity of the situation and the only logical recourse my business had to counter the unwillingness of certain customers to settle their accounts. I was within my rights to take whatever steps were necessary to collect the outstanding balances, now that the debtor had exhibited a reluctance to pay what he owed.

The more they screamed the calmer I became. After fifteen minutes of haranguing, each of the debtors agreed to come to the store today and settle up. I agreed to accept 75 cents on the dollar, if they agreed to pay the balance within thirty days. Two done deals. Jonteil had to drive to three job sites before noon to collect cash. She was not a happy soul when she returned.

"One of the sonsabitches called me a pantry girl and you a nigger lover. One wanted to know if I wanted to earn a tip from my knees. But, I got the money . . . all of it. I doubt if the three assholes will be buying from here again in the near future, until they're denied credit from the stores at the mall. If it weren't for the personal affronts, this project would be humorous. It is fun to confront a Skandahoovian and all his faux machismo while he is on the job, where he's supposed to be king. Then bring him to his knees by explaining what we will do to him if he doesn't pay. Aunt Jemima conquers Erik the Viking."

"Certainly no ethnic struggle there."

She smiled and went back to her telephone and I to mine. Denny Sorens of LakeFront Construction verbally carved me a new sphincter about eighteen inches north of my natural one. But, he agreed to give me his personal credit card number for half of what his company owed and promised to deliver the balance in two days. I've known Denny since we were in kindergarten. It hurt me almost as it hurt him. But, he had traded on our friendship and now it was business, and time to pay up. His credit card carried the amount. By the end of the day we had alienated everyone to whom we spoke, but we had collected twice the amount of last week's two-day effort. I felt sure Jonteil would discuss that day's event with Omar and he would deduce the something from our musings was becoming reality.

* *

His anxious voice on the answering machine on the kitchen counter confirmed my hunch. I returned his call.

"Bric, Jonteil told me about your day. She's in the tub now, so I can talk. What drove you to this intensity?"

"Tommy called this morning. All twenty-four of the shift managers are going to be casualties. His buddy Gus gave him a heads up. The threat is no longer on the horizon. It at the front door. We are about to embark upon a war of survival . . . mortal combat . . . and the first skirmish will be Friday. I am no longer frightened. I am resolved to self-preservation."

"Jesus, you're sounding like one of those survivalists or a neo-Nazi."

"I am a realist. Tommy is a realist. And, you should be one too. First general industry. Then the retail commerce. Then the governmental infrastructure. Like flu season, all people will suffer. We need to protect our selves and our loved ones. In this instance, protection is money. We need money and a lot of it. The strong will survive the cataclysm. Will you be strong?"

"Easy, big guy. Slow down. Remain calm. I heard some things, which may confirm your thinking. The Deputy Director sprang for lunch. I thought he was going to go over my performance review. Instead, he informed me that he was being called to St Paul for a planning meeting this Thursday. Planning meetings are budget meetings normally held during the ninth month of each year. This is obviously an emergency meeting. The only emergency I can see is budgetary. My guess is that all the work in the pipeline will be placed on long hiatus, and that each office will be asked to reallocate resources.

That's bureaucratic code for, in order of priority: eliminate overtime, cut salaries, let people go, and hire no replacements. Those, who are fortunate enough to survive, will have to work twice as hard for less money and diminishing security. He intimated that I should begin to explore alternative long-term career paths. He claimed he was getting pressure from St. Paul to become more cost-effective. Kids coming out of college are willing to work for a lot less than I make. The net of his innuendoes is that I'm fucked. So, I think you, Tommy, and I are all on the same page. But, we must be calm and plan with precision. My beloved is exiting her toilette. So I must cut short this conversation. Let's speak tomorrow."

My decision to call Tommy was made half way through Omar's assumptions.

* *

"Tommy, listen. I just got off the phone with Omar. He says the shit is about to hit the fan in his office. Most likely no layoffs . . . yet, but some severe belt-tightening. The time for us to act is now, before we all get swept away. Be at of the front of the caravan leaving the ghost town. Not the last ones, who turn off the lights. This is what I want you to do. I want you to concentrate on how we can acquire the funds. Sell property. Something. Where is there sufficient money for us? I'll do the same. Think of it as our retirement plan. Call me with any thoughts you have as soon as you have them."

Ellie is working her usual shift. I must sleep. Tomorrow will be more intense.

* *

Back to the telephones. Water from a stone would be easier than getting some of these deadbeats to pay. A few months ago we were sharing well wishes for Thanksgiving and whispering about Christmas shopping. Today, I am an AIDS victim who wishes to cut their flesh and spit in the wound. Money and debt kill relationships. But, I don't care what they think of me. They can rant all they want. I want my money and I want it now. Each conversation is an invective.

"Your dad was a better man than you'll ever be . . . Have you forgotten how much I spend at your store? . . . How the hell do your sleep at night? . . . You'll never do another dime's worth of business in this town . . . You want to put my kids on the street? . . ."

They scream and whine, but they know I'm right. They owe, so they must pay. Four of them promised to be here by six to settle. We'll see. Jonteil has another day of abuse, but she seems to get perverse pleasure from humiliating these men. She collects nearly four grand. She looks exhausted. I send her home at three. Tomorrow is the pay-or-else day.

The notices of payment due from our wholesalers are two-inches think on my desk. The light at the end of the tunnel may be a freight train or a beacon to guide me to safety.

"Bric, it's for you on line two."

"Bric, it's me, Tommy. I got it."

"Got what?"

"The source."

"The source?"

"Yeah, where we will acquire our retirement funds."

"Say no more. Can you come to the store now?"

"Sure, I'll be there in fifteen minutes."

Randy Mossman came by and gave me three grand. He agrees that the balance will be paid in sixty days. Then he wants to run a sixty-day tab. I agree. Tommy is standing in the door as Randy leaves. He enters the office and closes the door.

"Slicker than snot on the frozen lake. Gutsy and illegal, but easy. We get our funds from the bank truck that picks up cash from various retail merchants. I saw the truck at Nooners this morning and realized I had seen it there every Monday at roughly the same time . . . 10:15 AM. I don't know where the truck stops before it gets to Nooners. I do know its route after Nooners. I followed it until lunch. I figure the guys at the plant can't complain. Shit I'm going to be fired on Friday.

From Nooners, the truck goes to three other restaurants, and then the mall where it visits all the stores. After lunch I'm not positive, but I'd bet it continues making rounds until it's full. I drove past the Norst Bank downtown at three and there was no customer activity. So I parked behind the Dumpster in the back. About three-thirty the truck pulls up to the back entrance. The truck side door is opened and it sort of locks onto the building. A guy gets out and rings a buzzer at the door. About a minute later, the bank building door is opened so that the edge reaches the truck and is locked onto the vehicle.

The process creates a two-door metal tunnel through which the guard in the truck and one from the bank move the bags of money that have been picked up during the day. The entire door locking and money-unloading takes fifteen minutes. Then the two doors are unlocked and returned to their normal positions. The truck drives off to its parking spot in the garage. I figure with a full day of stops after a weekend there might be enough money in the bags to at least start us on our way. Just start, though. Like seed money. All we have to do is figure away to get the bags before they're taken into the bank."

"All we have to do is figure out a way to commit a robbery. Given the fact that the money is insured we will be taking money from the insurance company. So we won't be robbing from our friends. Good start, Tommy. Just a second, I have to answer the buzzer. I'm expecting some deposits of my own. Yes, thank you. If you would, please bring me the envelope. And could you stay until 6:30. I'm expecting another envelope."

I answer the knock on the door and take the fruits of my day's labor. The large manila envelope holds four grand. Another drop in the bucket.

"Tommy, given what you just told me, I'll take this to the bank personally tomorrow."

"But, Bric, you haven't heard the best part. Here is the icing on the cake. SpringFest Monday is coming in two weeks. And, the Friday before that is payday at the plant. That means there will be a really long, really big spending weekend. The stores will have all their summer merchandise on display. Families will shop and then go out to dinner as part of the celebration of winter's end. Traffic will be hell, but the money will flow. Lots of drinking, dining out, and shopping for four days . . . Friday noon through Monday evening. A real load of cash before the bank truck makes its rounds on Tuesday.

That's when we have to strike. I realize that doesn't give us much time to plan, but the take will be much larger that weekend than a regular Monday. It could be worth the push. Whadda' ya say, Bric, are your balls big enough?"

Tommy was on a roll. He never had it easy. His parent's divorce, failure to get into college, and the no-future job at the plant. He can be a nasty fighter on the basketball court. Now he was fighting for his life. His aggressive personality trait was fueling his fire. Nothing burns hotter than the threat of failure. There is no greater prize than success.

"Hey, man. Got to split. After my hard day of discovery, I want to spend some quiet time working on the details. Check with you tomorrow."

The buzzer rings. The second envelope has arrived. I am the last soldier at the fort. Time to count today's take. The most recent contribution is light. The sonofabitch will pay for not living up to our agreement. Total count for Monday and today is thirteen and a-half. Still very short of the minimum goal. A lot more work to do. Tomorrow I have to draft the letters and prepare the small space newspaper ad with all the names. Can't have second thoughts or waver. Must be resolute. My dad wavered with credit. The booze helped. It almost cost the store.

* *

"Bric, listen, Jonteil is at her aerobics class, so we can talk. Did you read the paper today?"

"Not yet."

"The lead story in the state section was about the State and Federal DEA guys taking credit for closing down the heroin market in the Twin Cities. They claim to have shut down two plants and three distribution systems, and confiscated nearly five million dollars worth of smack, coke and guns. Twelve arrests. I suspect they let the street punks walk after they rolled on the real dealers. Just nabbed the visible bad guys. My bet is that they wanted these guys to get to the guys who were shipping the shit into the market. You know, follow the chain up to the top. A great feather in the cap of the State DEA, if they can take credit for being the initiators of a massive shutdown. The feds will follow the path from Minneapolis to the source or sources."

"That's all well and good, but what does that have to do with us."

"The DEA, by closing down the processors and dealers, created a void, which can be filled by others. Face it. The government may take away drugs, but it can never take away addiction. The addicts will always be ready and willing to do whatever it takes to feed their habits. And, they are not choosy. They'll buy from anybody who has shit to sell. So the feds have created our opportunity. We can become the new suppliers to the Twin Cities. There is ready demand. We can be suppliers."

"That scenario has only a minor risk attached to it. I mean feeding near-insane junkies. Stepping between the junkies and their near-insane feeders. And doing all of this under the noses of the state and federal agents, I'd say there is a huge chance we could be shot or arrested . . . or both. Between life and death, I'll take life."

"Think of the risk-reward spectrum. The greater the risk, the greater the reward. Now consider this scenario. Whatever we get from our fiscal acquisition step could be doubled or tripled in value if we can convert the cash into heroin, then deal the smack in the Twin Cities."

"OK, now you've introduced another element of great risk. Assuming we can find a supply of heroin to buy, who's to say we won't get ripped off or killed for our cash? I mean it's not like we will be working with our aunts and uncles. The supply of smack will, no doubt, come from a source beyond our realm of present knowledge or influence. Strangers, who are as ruthless as we are naïve. Talk about lambs to slaughter. You have just painted a picture of ultimate risk and maximum opportunity for failure. Ours."

"Hear me out. I have a cousin who deals. He claims small time, but I think not so. He never thought small in his life. He lives in City of Industry, outside LA. I haven't spoken to him in a few years. Not since my aunt, his mother, died. But, I think I can still find him. I'm sure, for a cut or cash, he would be willing to connect for us. Or, better still, give us a name of a legitimate connection, who will sell to strangers on his say so. This will reduce the risk substantially. Then, after we make the buy, we can move it to the Twin Cities. Unload it for a big profit and go underground with real money."

"That's really scary. Too many possibilities for failure or death. We need to think about this long and hard. We may have the seed money cash source and there is real risk there. Now, you claim to have found a way to increase the value of any cash we might get. We need to discuss all the details and I mean all the details. Can we meet tomorrow night? Here, at my place? Ellie will be working. I'll call Tommy. Say at seven. No, better yet, lets meet at the boat. That way we have absolute privacy. Seven at the boat, OK?"

"See you then, partner."

* *

Wednesday is the final reckoning for our deadbeat customers. Jonteil and I make our calls and remind those who have the courage to answer the phones that five PM is the deadline. If they choose not to pay, their names will appear in an ad in the newspaper and their businesses will be noted as having failed to pay debts. Notification will go to both the Better Business Bureau and the Chamber of Commerce.

This three-pronged attack will not only make it almost impossible for them to buy on account anywhere, it will also make potential customers wary about fronting them money for materials. Customers will fear that money is not being used properly and that misuse may cause the job to be stopped before completion. Basically, the deadbeats will be fucked from front and back. Very shortly the same men who thought they could make a fool of me will be out of business. Better them than me.

Jonteil and I encounter greater hostility that previously. The condemned are crying on the walk to the chair. I hear her say, *"We're open until five, if you want to stay alive."* By four-thirty we have been visited by several cranky craftsmen. The net of our efforts is that we have received enough money to pay some wholesalers, some sales tax, and some operating expenses for the next month. Then we have to scramble all over again. This second round of scrambling will exclude those, whom we have sentenced to the perdition of non-payment. Thirty days should be enough time for most of the wounds to heal and our paying customer base to return. Only eight customers will be held up for public ridicule. They will receive letters of our actions in tomorrow's mail. I will deposit the cash Friday with the rest of the week's bounty. Jonteil heads for home and I for the boat . . . aptly named, *Treasure Chest*.

* *

"I call to order the second meeting of the Get-out-of Dodge-and-Get-Rich-Quick gang. Do we have any old business? The chair recognizes Tommy Bowen."

Tommy repeats his discovery and the need for swift action.

"The chair recognizes Omar Williams."

Omar repeats his plan for wealth augmentation.

"Do we have any new business? Thomas Bowen."

"I figure we'll need hand guns and cans of mace to spray in the eyes of truck guards. Blind them before the recognize us. I figure we'll need some form of get away vehicle that is not ours or traceable. I figure we'll need masks, gloves, and coveralls like they wear at the gas stations. So our identities are completely disguised. No offense, Omar, but you are recognizable. I figure we'll need a place to go when we leave town. I haven't worked through that one yet."

"The Chair recognizes Mr. Williams."

"I spoke to my cousin, and after the usual bullshit of denial, he allowed he had heard of some people in Albuquerque, who might be able to accommodate us. He wants a finder's fee of ten grand. That seems unreasonable, but negotiable. He told me the going rate for Black Tar heroin uncut was 20 grand a kilo. Maybe less if we bought a lot. A kilo could be stepped on, that's diluted, to produce two times the volume. That's two kees. Then one of the kees is repackaged in one-gram packets, which could be sold to a dealer for fifty dollars each. The uncut kee is sold for 40 grand. We can charge a premium for the packaged shit, because the stuff is ready to move. The dealers have no overhead. They charge what the market will bear . . . $60 or $70 a packet. Maybe more if the market is dry. So from each $20,000 invested in a kilo, we get $90,000. If we can buy 9 kilos we can gross 800 grand or more. Net of 300 grand per couple. Cash money. Enough for a clean start somewhere.

I think the price per gram can be higher, because the junkies in the Twin Cities have been cut off. The longer they are without, the more we can make. Let's say there's 200 grand in the truck and we can buy 9 kees. We'll need 20 grand for traveling expenses. Then step on the six, to make them twelve. Then move that. Bingo, instant money. And that's conservative. The more money there is in the truck and the more the junkies are willing to pay, the more we can make."

My pulse was pounding. The light in the tunnel was not moving toward me. I was going to the light. It was my turn.

"The escape I have in mind is almost as good as your parts of the plan. I developed it knowing we would have to go to get the money out of state, just not where. After we hit the truck, we split three ways. Tommy, you'll go to the peninsula and board a seaplane for a flight to Canada, the reservation for the last flight of the day has to be made soon. You'll just be one of the six passengers. Once in Canada, you get to a local airport and board a flight to Phoenix.

You going to Canada will not raise any suspicion, because you have relatives about twenty-five miles from the seaport in Ontario. I get Omar home. He then takes a taxi to the airport and boards a plane to the Twin Cities then Tampa, Florida for a convention. I will drive to the Twin Cities in an old junker, the one behind my cabin. It had served its usefulness, but somehow I couldn't part with it after these years. I just left it parked in the lean-to with the firewood and yard tools.

We will use the junker as the getaway car. My flight from there will take me to Denver ostensibly for some skiing. We will leave these three interim destinations and meet in

Albuquerque at some motel. That's how we get away. Now we have the three ingredients. What's next?"

* *

The silence was overpowering. No one even moved. We were frozen by the enormity of the moment. We had to be absolutely, flat-out positive we wanted to do this thing. Up to now our conversations were pipe dreams. We had committed no criminal act. Now we were standing on the edge of the cliff. If we went further, we would give up our life of freedom and pursue the path of crime. If we took one more step, we could not turn back. Were we committed? Were our words more than drug-induced chatter? Bravado? Were they truly precursors to deeds? Were the words motivated by a frustration with our present life and the fear of immediate financial failure.

Was the way out of the trap to embark upon a real hard-edged adventure? Were we modern-day *Long Riders*, driven by economics not of our own doing to a life of crime? Or was this a romantic fantasy of righting a personal affront. My rationalization was that we had a safety net. If caught, we could wiggle out of long jail time. We'd return the money, if we were caught before we bought the drugs. Or, we would cooperate with the authorities by rolling on the suppliers in Albuquerque and the dealers in Minneapolis.

A big insurance policy. But, given the vagaries of the legal system, this escape was based on a lot of precedent. The real danger was in the acts themselves. The guards had guns and senses of duty. The sellers had guns and their own rules of business conduct. Plus, no scruples. The buyers had guns and a different set of rules. Again, no scruples. So, our plan was, bottom-line, extremely dangerous.

* *

"Fuck it, Bric, we'll do it. For a quarter of a million dollars, I'd kill. That's more money than I ever dreamed of. Besides, I've got nothing to lose. This town is a dead end. We can pull it off. Gettin' the money will be easy and turn into to drugs won't be that tough with Omar's introduction. Then we leave for some great island in the Caribbean. Some place that has no extradition arrangement with this country. Like the place where Vesco went."

"I'm in, Tommy. If my stupid-ass cousin has avoided jail for all these years, his Ivy League educated cousin can do the crime and not do the time. Besides every homie wants to be a gangster. Not a merry motherfuckin' nigger prankster."

As simple as that. Three middle class men had agreed that becoming criminals was better than suffering *the slings and arrows of outrageous fortune. And, by opposing, end them.*

"Then we're in. No turning back. From now on, we have to take small, but rapid steps. While we are working out the details of the events, we must also think about the ladies. If they are with us, we are a go . . . no sweat. If they are against the plan, we are fucked. We can't not tell them. Once they know what we want to do, it will be tough to do it without their support. If we try to do it without them, they'll take the heat. The cops will find us through them. As much as they may love us, they will roll on us to save their own asses. So, now the three of us face more decisions. How do we tell them to enlist their involvement? How do we convince them that this action is in their best interests?

Listen, you guys. If we can see that this is the only way to go, they will see it, too."

"Tommy, it's more romantic for three guys to consider crime, than for three women. It's been that way for centuries. Men were the rapers and pillagers."

"Bric, not always. Think of the Viking woman, and the female tribal leaders of the Amazon."

"Let's hope you're right."

"Let's have a meeting tomorrow at my place. When does Ellie get off her shift?"

"Thursday is the strange day, Omar . . . she works from eleven 'til seven."

"Good. Then the six of us will meet at my place tomorrow at 8:30. To drink and sit in the hot tub. I'll talk to Jonteil before you all arrive. Circumspect and very vague. By the time you all arrive, I'll know what she feels. We can take it from there. If she is horrified by the idea, it's a dead issue, and we'll have to decide to either abandon our plans or our wives. But, if she is can-do, we are a-go. The next step comes down to the decision of the three ladies."

"OK, that's settled. Between now and then, the three of us have to make notes covering all the specific items and actions we will need to take. The plan has to be tight. Very, very tight. No loose ends to unravel. Loose ends cause failure. Here is the way to do that. Each of us will take the point-of-view that he alone will commit the deeds, and that he alone is responsible for all the details. If the ladies are in agreement with our program, we will share the three variations, and ask for their input. I'm sure each of us will have missed some detail thought of by the others. I am equally sure the ladies will think of things each one of us missed. After tomorrow night, we will have a master plan with the input of only three or shared with all six. Tomorrow is it."

Leaving Ellie would be difficult, but not impossible. Both of us would get over the end of our relationship. I would be in the Caribbean and she could find another guy to share her life. Leaving a sweetheart is emotionally wrenching. Leaving a wife can be emotionally destructive. But both acts are not earth shattering, because neither a sweetheart nor wife is blood. The commitment made to a wife or sweetheart is really an arrangement with a giant "get out of jail free" clause. Leaving a child or a parent is entirely different. The commitment to a child or parent is permanent. It is a sacred bond, which cannot be broken. That's one of life's rules.

THURSDAY'S CHILD

Omar and Jonteil's house is on the ridge that overlooks the lake about fifteen miles east of town. The trip goes from main road to narrow black top, to long dirt driveway. Back in the woods, they and we are safe from prying eyes and ears.

"This is a nice break, Bric. As I remember, the views from all the rooms are terrific. I feel guilty we didn't bring anything."

"Ellie, said it was their treat. A sort of a bounce back for the days on the boat. Tommy and Marilee will be here, too."

In an open shed, behind the house is the John Deere necessary to maintain the three acres and long drive way. Mower, earth plow and snow plow . . . different attachments for different seasons sit quietly beside their motorized better half. Because Ellie was late getting relieved at the hospital, we are the last to arrive.

Up the steps to the back porch and the thermo-paned doors. Before we can knock, Omar slides open the panel, he deeply bows and we make a grand entrance. The sweet smell of party fills the air.

"Enter honored guest. Allow me to announce your arrival."

"Ladies and gentlemen, I have the honor to introduce . . ."

The shouts from Jonteil, Tommy, and Marilee drowned out the pomposity of the party steward.

"Hey, baby what's up."

"Jonteil, you look great. I'm sorry, but working with you everyday, I overlook how attractive you are."

"Easy, Bric. You comin' on to my lady and you ain't even toked. Baby, watch your ass when he gets high. Better yet, I'll watch your ass."

"What about me, Bric?"

"Marilee, I don't work with you. I've already made a fool of myself and I just got here. So, I'll hold off commenting for a while."

"Ellie, where did your get that dress? Did you bring your suit for the tub? After a while I want to show you and Marilee the cute outfits I bought last weekend."

Jonteil was in her take-charge groove. She never lacked for assertiveness. Sometimes I thought she wore the pants in her marriage. Omar could be passive. Maybe that was his aggression. The three women drifted into the kitchen. The three men drifted to the front porch. It was a cold clear lakeside night. The hot tub bubbled and the black sky glistened with twinklers and the half moon. Good single-malt Scotch whisky in one hand, the other remained free to accept, enjoy and pass the joint fired-up by Omar.

"Guys, here's the deal. I sorta hinted around our idea to Jonteil. She asked a ton of questions, all of which I sidestepped. Told her they would all be answered when the six of us were together. She seemed to get excited. I'm not sure if was the idea of doing something dramatic and dangerous or just the weed. But, she wants to hear what we have to say."

"I talked to Marilee on the way over. You know, about our jobs and our limited futures. She told me she was sick and tired of doing the same shit every day and every year with no control over her life. She wants to do something new and different. I'm not sure she's thinking of what we have in mind, but I know she will listen. And she is dutiful. She's my gal. So I'm confident, she'll go along."

"Ellie has no clue. She has bitched about the demands on her life that the ER is making. Staff reductions and the longer hours. Delayed delivery of equipment and the inconveniences that means. I'm not sure she is thinking about tossing in the towel. But, she is not a happy camper."

"Then it's agreed. Tonight, here and now, we show them ours and hope they will show us theirs."

* *

Driven by the whisky and the tokes, my mind is racing along six different scenarios at once. Sometimes overlapping. Sometimes going off on a tangent so far out that I forgot where I am or was going. Sipping, smoking and dreaming, I'm independent of the others yet connected by purpose. We are seated in the pit, a three-quarters arc of padded bench and back that nearly surrounds the fire. Between the bench and the fireplace is a wrought-iron table, with a polyurethaned hardwood top. The table stand has several drawers, which hold napkins, matches, and all sort of paraphernalia needed for outdoor enjoyment. Beyond the fireplace, the lake and its enormity are visible. An unobstructed view for about forever.

The fire crackles; sparks rise, and flames sensually lick the sky. Omar designed the fireplace for maximum heat radiation with minimum fuel consumption. It's all metal skin, top, bottom and sides, will glow after about 30 minutes of burning. The grate sits twelve inches over a concave the base, the heater is about six feet in diameter, but the metal cap is only three feet above the grate. Ash removal is from the back end. Quite appropriate. He has his logs cut to the precise length. The do not overlap the grate. The fuel supply is kept in a hardwood chest, which has metal shelving to allow for stacking and drying of the logs. This fireplace has been engineered to the nines.

There is the hint of spring and geo-rebirth in the air. The nights take a little longer to envelop the days and the air is just a tad warmer each week. These are obvious signs to everyone. But, I notice is the smell. The night air smells different. No flowers and no green leaves to make the air smell better. The fresh aroma means that the snow and moisture of winter are no longer stultifying the olfactory sense. I can smell rain before the first lightening and snow before the wind gusts. The bromine odor emanating from the hot tub cannot mask the newness of the night air.

* *

The sliding of the doors severs my reverie. Jonteil has negotiated the food and drink wagon easily over the bottom part of the door's frame. Omar designed small ramps to facilitate transportation from inside out and vice versa. Another use of his talent at home.

"Who wants another drink, or smoke, or, and here is a novel idea, some food. We have lots of everything. The meal consists of appetizers. Hors d'oeuvres for all. I said we would treat, not that I would cook. I don't do kitchen well. Ask Omar. I am going to have another drink, before I dilute the good whisky with edibles. And, for sure one more big hit. Help yourself, everybody."

Little plates are piled high are the result of the munchies. Glasses are re-loaded as if we had to drink everything before the Canadians stormed the castle and took our whisky. Fluid, which should be a rich amber brown, looks more like weak tea. Chewing, sipping, and inhaling are our contribution to the night's symphony. For about ten minutes there is no conversation as we sate our primal urges.

"Well, is someone going to tell me why we are here? What is this big secret you guys have cooked up?"

"What secret?"

"Ellie, the little boys are so excited about telling us something they are about to chub up."

"Bric, what is Jonteil talking about?"

"Marilee, did Tommy say anything to you recently. I mean anything strange or out of the ordinary."

"Well, he was bitching about his life and that he would rather be somewhere else doing anything else. But, ever since he told me about the plant layoffs and how he feared for the future of his job, he has been worried. I understand that."

"Sweetie, they told me I would be laid off tomorrow. I was waiting for a good time to tell you and this is it."

Marilee's face went ashen as she stopped chewing.

"Those rotten motherfuckers. After all you have done for the company. The timesaving programs you introduced. The hours of overtime without overtime pay. The Saturdays. And now they can you. Why you? It's just not fair. What will we do? How will we manage? I mean we have some savings, but not enough to live on. How do they expect us to live? Those rotten motherfuckers."

"Honey, relax all that doesn't matter anymore. Bric, Omar and I have an idea."

"Bric, what's going on?"

"Ellie, remember how I was convinced the financial apocalypse was about to happen. Sadly, I was right. The store may not get out of the toilet. Despite the hard work of Jonteil and me, the deadbeats may pull the store down. Money is so fucking scarce and our suppliers are no longer sympathetic. Soon I will have to consider layoffs or part time work for the people at the store. Maybe selling the store property just to pay off the debts. That assumes I could find a buyer looking to rehab bad property. You even said you see the financial crunch at the ER with staff and equipment. How much can the hospital cut without hurting service? They can demand that you all work lots of over time without pay or time off until something terrible happens. Well, the three of us have an idea. A plan to get the six of us out of the dumper. It will take full and immediate cooperative teamwork from all of us, but the plan can work. We can get out of Dodge before the banker forecloses on the ranch."

* *

With that, we laid out the details of our idea: Tommy the acquisition and timing, I the escape, and Omar the finances. The women were speechless.

"Omar, that's it? That's really scary and totally risky."

"That's the over view, we need to get all the details in place. We're working on them all the time. Tying up the loose ends can eliminate the risk."

"Honey, you got a lot of details to consider. More than the three of you can handle. I mean, how do you keep the local cops from catching you. How reliable is your cousin's connection, and whom do you plan to contact in Minneapolis to push the shit onto the street? Those are big details. Each one of them has hundreds of small details, any one of which can trip you up. You're going to need help and a lot of it."

"Jonteil, I take it your in."

"Look, the way I see it, we could stay here and go through our day-to-day existences and be controlled by the decisions of others or we could do something for ourselves by ourselves. My livelihood presently depends on Bric and his store. If the store goes under at the time of the plant layoffs, I'll be on the street with all the white folks. In that scenario, who's going to hire and well-educated, pushy black woman? Omar and I are no Bonnie and Clyde, but we can stand on our own. Your plan has many elements of risk and a big reward. I can help reduce the risk to get my share of the reward. But, we must always have an out. A safety net as we go along this path. What I mean is we must plan for the real possibility that we could be caught. If we are caught, we must be prepared and to lighten our load by giving up the money or the sellers or dealers. Preferably both."

"Bric, honey, my first concern is that we don't get hurt. What if the bank guards want to do their duty and defend the money in the truck? What if Omar's cousin's friends in Albuquerque try to rip us off? What if the dealers in Minneapolis try to rip us off? There are too many instances where someone could get killed."

"Ellie, we'll be on the guards so fast and so hard they won't be able to respond. We'll pepper spray them. Besides, they're too old to do anything. I'm sure they're trained to let the money go rather than fight to protect it. The complete acquisition will be over in less than two minutes. Then to the purchase, Omar said his cousin would meet us in Albuquerque to introduce us to the Mexicans and to get his finder's fee. We have to work hard to get a connection in Minneapolis. Some one we can trust. Some one who has access to a lot of cash. I don't give a fuck how he gets rid of the shit. That will be his problem. Marilee, what do you have to say?"

"Frightening. Exciting, but frightening. Exhilaratingly frightening. I don't know whether it's the smoke or the booze, but I like the idea. We can do it. Has anybody thought of what we do after we unload the heroin in Minneapolis? It won't take too long before the cops figure out that we took the money. I mean when the six of us are missing from Duluth at the same time as the robbery, they'll start to trace our trips. They'll track us to Albuquerque and then Minneapolis. I'm sure they'll alert the authorities of our activities. We have to hit Minneapolis and get out before anyone but the buyer knows we are there. Then where do we go?"

"We can go to one of the small islands in the Caribbean. There are some of them that don't want to be bothered returning American citizens. Hell, we'll probably be celebrities. We'll have cash and no place to spend it, but in the local economy. Or, we can split up and fend for ourselves. Find some small towns out West or in the Deep South where we can hide in plain sight. The possibilities are endless."

Return to dead calm for two or three minutes. Soul searching silence. This is the cutting edge. In or out. Go or stop. No one wants to be the next to speak, except me.

"The deal is quite simple. We can't do this without you ladies. If we were to rob the truck and leave the state you would be in jeopardy. The cops would be all over you to get to us. They could threaten you with jail time if you don't talk. The odds of us being caught would increase to 100%. So, if you are with us, it will be done. If you are not, I don't know what we'll do."

The three keepers of destiny glance at each other, at us, and then each other. Their countenances are mixtures of curiosity and panic. Their silence last for a year.

"I'll get pads of paper and pens. We'll need to write down all we can, like what is needed, who gets it, what to do, and when to do it. All the damned details."

"Jonteil, are you sure?

"I'm sure, Ellie. Marilee?"

"If you two are sure, I'm sure, as long as we have escape hatches."

So, the post-meal madness commences. There are certain similar things that we all have to do will do for the public's eyes: setting up vacations, gathering money for expenses, and arranging trips. There are specific responsibilities, our new job related responsibilities that we must accomplish to make sure the process runs smoothly.

Jonteil plans a car accident near the border of the city and county. This will draw both city and county police and keep them busy while we are removing the funds from the truck and fleeing.

Marilee says that she can park the around the corner from the bank's rear entrance, so that no one will have the vaguest idea where we went. The impression will be that the three of us dispersed into the downtown crowd and disappeared. After we get rid of the clown suits.

Ellie knows a former nurse, now administrator, in the Twin Cities who, she thinks, is into recreational drugs. She peddles what she can lift from the hospital for cash to buy coke and, maybe, smack. She will get in touch with her to get some names of upper level dealers, who could handle our heroin. She will probably have to drive to Minneapolis for a sit down to get the information.

Tommy has already bought his disguise items. Three full headed clown masks, orange jump suits, and white cotton gloves. The disguises and not the bodies inside them will stick in anyone's mind. Anyone who sees us will think we are leftovers from SpringFest. Be sure to wear sneakers. He says tomorrow is his last day and his first day.

We can buy the merchandise we need to prep the smack for sale in various stores in Albuquerque.

Omar will confirm all the details about Albuquerque with his cousin. Asks if it would be wise to have his cousin meet us and be there when we buy. He could help us with the chemistry of dilution. But, he'll definitely want more than ten grand. When he sees the size of our finished product, he'll probably try to extort another twenty. Maybe we should pay him with product.

Jonteil asks about ID's. After we do the deed, we'll need new ID's. We won't have time to get them in Minneapolis, so somewhere before then, we'll need to change our identities. Omar will ask his cousin. More money.

Marilee asks how what we plan to do with the bags and the stuff inside we can't use. Decided. Open the bank bags at a safe place. Parking lot by the auditorium. Always cars left there. Transfer all the large bills to three other bags . . . one for each traveler. Dump the checks, small bills, paper work, bank bags, coveralls, and masks in the trunk of the junker. Keep gloves on until the very end of our departure. Cops will find the small bills, and they can send alerts about larger bills to banks across the country. We'll have to count and wrap in Albuquerque. Our three bags will be large canvas types with locks. Checked in at each airport.

Marilee can't get vacation time so quickly. She will have to visit her sick mother in St. Louis for a few days. Mom slipped and broke her hip. Dad incapable of dealing with crisis or getting her home from the hospital. Only child needs a few days to set up the home care.

Ellie's vacation is long overdue. She has accumulated about five weeks of compensatory time. The hospital doesn't pay overtime. It rewards the extra hours with additional time off, which no one can ever take. It's a great system.

* *

As the details unfold, my mind begins to jump with excitement. Can we think of every contingency? We can do this. What have we forgotten? Break the event into sections. Acquisition. Departure. Arrival. Purchase. Delivery. Permanent departure. It has to be seamless and non-violent. Carry guns to talk the talk. Just can't walk the walk.

Ellie's idea of not liquidating all assets is good. Take money from savings and checking for our expenses. Leave some in the bank so as not to arouse suspicion before and immediately after the event. She figures we will have a forty-eight to ninety-six hour head start. The better our plan the longer it will take the authorities to connect the dots. The sparser our trail the greater the chance for escape.

What about the get away car? The Dodge. The old piece-of-crap will require at least new tires and battery. It's been up on blocks. Sort of suspended animation for years. Awaiting a return to life. Only after the battery is installed can I know if it will turn over and run. My guess is that running will not be a problem. Running smoothly is out of the question. I'll know by tomorrow night. Easy to purchase any needed parts from a junkyard. Lots of dead relatives resting at the junkyard. No one has seen the car for five years and the gaping maws of rust will act as camouflage. It will look just like another Skandahoovian sled, down from the woods for summer supplies. No one will take special notice.

The questions, answers and comments were coming at such a rate and with no order. It was tough to keep up. We all asked others to repeat. The drugs clouded and expanded our minds. Concentration was often difficult. We would take a point and push it to an extreme, and to look at it from each point of view; ours, the cops, and those with whom we would be in contact. Anticipation of every contingency would be the key to our success. No telling how long the Q&A session went on. The food was devoured, bottles emptied, and two more joints were passed. We were cramming for the final exam of our lives.

* *

"I quit."

"Me, too. I'm exhausted."

"My mind is frazzled. I can't concentrate."

"Let's break. Anyone for the tub? I'm going to become a prune."

"Let's all go. Ellie and I will get the dregs into the kitchen. Marilee, why don't you get the towels and the Terri robes? They're in the laundry room. You big strong, wise men can clean up this mess, stoke the fire, and make sure the tub is ready for us. Just one rule: Suits are permitted, just not required."

"Jonteil, you say that every time we're here. We know the rules and the reality."

The ladies go about their chores and we ours.

"Bric, that was great. I really thought we were going to have to work hard to convince them. Jonteil took charge. Ellie and Marilee trusted her lead. Shows you how little we know about them."

"Omar, I guess every girl wants to be a gangster and not a merry motherfuckin' nigger prankster. I trust you two, and I love Ellie. I hope the interest the three of them showed tonight will carry through. I think it is our best interests to probe their commitment this weekend. Make sure it's not the whisky and smoke that's talking. If we spot a weakness in their resolve, we can still kill the plan."

"I know Marilee is committed. If she didn't want to do this thing, she would have let all of us know right away. Here and now. That's the bottom line with her. Jesus, I'm getting so excited I gettin' wood. Hey, where can we change?"

"In the shower room over there, where we always change. Please take a pee before you get in the tub. Bric and I will load the fire and take drink tray over to the bubbling caldron of relaxation."

Tommy, quick walks his way to change. We complete our tasks, undress, and get into our swim trunks. I glance at my watch. It's only 9:45. God, I would have given odds it was near midnight. Keeping track of time is impossible when the brain is chugging and churning. Still, there is a lot to be done immediately, and our days will be long for the next two weeks. So, Ellie and I should leave around eleven. Maybe I won't deposit the cash Jonteil and I extracted this week. That will be part of our travelling purse. Only Jonteil and I know how much there is, and she and I aren't coming back. Suddenly, I feel a twinge of concern for my store and the employees, who will be left on the beach. Just as suddenly the film of moral correctness is washed away by the hope of my better future.

"OK, girls, here we come, ready or not."

They are not. Tommy and Marilee are alone in the tub. They are necking and rubbing. Marilee is the obvious aggressor. Tommy is just there. She is siting on Tommy's lap facing him. Who knows where her hands are? Or any other body extension for that matter. God, you leave kids alone for five minutes and they rut.

"Excuse us, you two. Is it safe to enter the love pond? I mean Bric and I don't want cause *coitus interruptus* by the gyrating couple. Normally, we'd throw cold water on you, but I be damned if I'll waste my drink."

"Sorry. I just got caught up in the moment."

"Yes, daddy, we'll wait 'til we get home or maybe just the car."

They awkwardly separate and Marilee adjusts her suit.

"Hey, what did we miss? You two puttin' on a show for our men? Getting them all hot and bothered or just adding personal foam to the broth?"

"Omar and I thought you guys were never going to make an entrance. We were being entertained while we waited."

"We have something special to show you all. After Christmas, Ellie and I ordered special outfits for the hot tub. Now close your eyes . . . all of you. Viola."

There they stood in matching bikinis ordered from Victoria's Secret. The three triangles created the impression of modesty. When Jonteil moved, the impression disappeared. There was a sliver of silver fabric pretending to be a thong. Ellie's nipples were visible in the cold air. Both girls had shaved or used depilatories. The sight was electrifying. There is much to be said about the illusion of pre-pubescence. But, in polite society it is better left unsaid.

"Ellie, you look terrific."

"It's OK, Bric, you can comment about how I look. I know you are my boss, or were until tonight. Now we are partners. How do I look?"

"Honey, you look good enough to . . ."

"I asked Bric."

"Absolutely stunning. I would have never guessed underneath all the work clothes and the one-piece bathing suit you always wear when we are here there was that kind of body. I don't mean to be rude, but Omar, you be one lucky dude."

The twins slipped into the tub. We all got comfortable.

"No peeing in the tub. If you have to go, get out and use the commode in the shower room. OK?"

"Yes, mother."

This was the Jonteil I knew. The time drifted away as the drinks disappeared. We giggled and dreamt out loud. What would we do with the money? Where would we go? Could the deed be repeated elsewhere? We were heady with success and we haven't done anything.

Ellie and I headed home at 11:15. Our lovemaking, always assertive after a time in Omar's tub, was particularly aggressive tonight. Ellie was much more than a willing participant, she wanted more than I did, but I gave her everything I had. Sleep for me was leaden.

Freaky Friday

Payday for the employees. They all want cash. Cash it's been for two generations and cash it is. I go to the bank at lunch and get funds to match the pay stubs, which match the hours. Put the right amount of money and a stub in each little brown envelope. Little brown envelopes are a hold over from forty years ago. I suspect some of the guys like cash because they can hold out some "own" money from their wives. That's another issue. After I drop off the envelopes with the guys, I'll head over to the auto parts store for a battery. Then out to the cabin. Cabin keys are at the house. In the kitchen cabinet there is a drawer that holds everything that meets the qualification of "we might need this later".

* *

In my desk is the large manila envelope, which contains the fruits of the weeks' calls and visits. $25,652. Half of it will be deposited to give the impression of business operations. The bills in the "To Pay" folder total over $81,000. I was right; we'd never get out of this mess legitimately. Jonteil has cut a check to pay the sales tax. She even provided a stamped envelope. I just sign and send. Another stalling tactic. Shit, sometimes I feel like the rearguard . . . just stall long enough for the army to escape.

"Bric, I'm going to take a long lunch. I need to do some shopping for resort wear. Then I'm going to visit some of our customers and see if I can hammer more money from them. It's payday all around, ya know."

"You are relentless. Let's make this a short day. I'll be out all afternoon. Up at the cabin doing some auto repair. I'll tell Jenny and Bill to close up at three or four depending on customer flow. Since they have the Saturday hours, an early close is only fair. Last night was really great. You and Omar put out a great spread. Thanks a lot."

We return to our tasks. Reading the notes from last night. My handwriting and sentence structure are somewhat jumbled. But, it's mine so I can decipher the ganja code. Must order the three bags from L.L. Bean. Winter catalog number LG-456-L in brown.

Skiers carry all. Guaranteed to hold everything needed for a week on the slopes except skis. Made from XXL gauge sail canvass and wrapped with three straps, riveted to the bottom fiberglass plate on the bottom. The straps and the double-sized double-fold handle are secured with combination locks for security. Sale price: $289.00. Standard delivery included, two-day delivery is $20.00.

Ordering on the Internet is everything they say it is, simple and built on trust. I trust LL.

"Bric, the call on line three is for you."

"Bric, Omar. I awakened my cousin to ask about the items we discussed last night. He told me he could deliver what we wanted, but he would need current color headshots just like on the real licenses. The photos have to have a light blue background. We need to get these photos to him by Tuesday. He will supply a driver's license, a Social Security card and a Voter's ID for each of us. L.A address. He'll have them in Albuquerque for us to sign a laminate. He wants five grand from each of us. And, he wants half in cash with the photos. Plus, he wants another five each for three guns that are clean and scraped, and five for the cutting base. You know the stuff to dilute the smack. He claims he is giving us the family discount.

I trust him about delivery. Not sure about price. The total he wants from us is thirty-five thousand . . . half of the ID cost and all of the money for the guns and powder. That's twelve per couple. We don't have much choice. We'll use my Christmas gift to take the pictures tomorrow morning. Can we use your blue living room curtains as background? I'll take the negatives to *See What Develops* up at the mall and get the shots back in the afternoon. If there are no glitches, we can send the shots and cash over night on Monday. OK?"

"Sounds like a plan. I can do the cash. No problem."

"So can I. I'm not sure about Tommy."

"Omar, think a little. He's getting a severance check today one week for every year and cash for his unused vacation. He'll just have to consider this a prepayment on his extended vacation. I'll call him when we hang up to make sure he cashes the check."

"What time tomorrow should we enjoy our Avedon experience?"

"Ten."

"See you then."

* *

"Tommy, I'm glad I reached you. By the way what are you doing in your office?"

"Just boxing my personal possessions. I got called to the boardroom about two hours ago. They read the legal song and dance. I suspect everything was recorded for their protection. I had to sign a bunch of papers. They signed them, too and gave me copies of everything. They handed me two checks. One for my time and one for accrued, unused benefits. They asked me to clean out my office, turn in my badge, and vacate the premises by noon. They have a security guard posted at the door to my office to make sure I don't destroy or steal any company property. The entire process is almost up lifting. Out of the muck and into the light, ya know."

"I know it must be tough, but it was no surprise. So hang tough, buddy. I just got off the phone with Omar. He spoke to his cousin, about the items we would need, ID's, guns and powder to cut the smack. His cousin says no sweat for the price. We have to supply pictures and some up front bread. Half the total, two and a half each. That's five per couple. Plus, another five for your gun and two for the other item. Your total is twelve. So, don't deposit your stipend. We need to send the shots and all the bread to the cousin on Monday. We will take the photos at my place tomorrow at ten. OK?"

"Fuck. Twelve large. There goes my last reward. Let me look at the checks again. Jesus, uncle sugar got is ton of flesh. Let me figure this. He took out 50%. That leaves me forty-eight hundred short. What can I do? I can't face Marilee and tell her I don't have enough money to make the plan work for us. The T&M Retirement Fund is in serious jeopardy."

"I'll front you the cash. You can pay me back after the deal. See you tomorrow at ten."

* *

I didn't realize his finances were so tight. Tighter than mine. What does he think Marilee thinks about their finances? Does she know how broke they are? Apparently not. Why can't he face her? What is he hiding beyond fiscal malfeasance? Drugs? Gambling at the Reservation Casino?

Now, to my chores. It's strange going into the bank today. Sort of like casing the joint. Except today I enter the font door and soon I'll be at the back door. Mrs. Farnsworth is awaiting my arrival. I hand her pay stubs and envelopes and await her return. Except for pleasantries about the weather, we have nothing to say during this business transaction. As usual, she is prompt in her return. I leave. Stop by the store and hand over the brown envelopes to Jenny. She is appreciative of the early close. Now to my house.

The sun heats the car's air, so I roll down my window. The fresh air reminds me that winter has not yet retreated. Pull into my driveway, I notice Jonteil's car. Did she go clothes shopping with Ellie? I'll bet they are modeling their new outfits for each other like a couple of teens. I'll just get the cabin key and let little girls be little girls.

The drawer is our answer to *Fibber Magee's* closet, except it doesn't spew forth its contents every time it's opened. But, there is so much stuff in it. Three types of string, two types of tape, bandages, burn ointment, cotton pad, air pump nozzle, box matches, pack matches, bottle opener, pencils, pens, envelopes, scraps of paper, receipts, warrantees for the blender and the toaster oven, stubs of candles, a small flashlight, assorted batteries . . . no two the same size, screw driver, pen knife, house keys, car keys and cabin keys. What you need is always on the bottom or in the way back. I wonder if the stuff moves when we are not looking. Does the drawer know what the next person will want and move that object to the back and beneath everything else?

I hear music coming from upstairs. The girls. I'll just sneak a peek at the fashion show. Like a cat, I climb the stairs, turn at the newel post, and slide down the hall. There is music, but no giggles emanating from the bedroom. I push open the door and see no one posing with today's finery. I am struck by a bolt of reality. There on the bed in a mutually gratifying head-to-thigh embrace are Ellie and Jonteil. Enmeshed in each other and oblivious to my presence. There is a part of me that is genuinely excited.

Every young man's fantasy is playing out on my bed. This part wants to leap out of my clothes and join in the fun. There is another, older part, that wants to scream, confront, then run away. It's not fun to see my lover in the arms of another. This means I am second fiddle. It is doubly hurtful that the other lover is a woman. This trivializes my manhood. Has Ellie been faking it with me? For how long? Is she bi-sexual? Is this her dalliance and I am real or is it vice versa? Is this the more she needs to be whole?

Does Omar know? Should I tell him? What if he doesn't care? What if he encourages Jonteil's exploration? Maybe he's doing them both at the same time. I can hear my heart, but not my breathing. I can't deal with this overwhelming personal issue now. I have objective car issues to resolve. I'll stay awake until Ellie gets home after her shift tonight. Then we'll talk. Tomorrow I'll talk to Omar. Maybe, I should just keep my mouth shut for the next few weeks. I can't let anything jeopardize the plan, which is in irrevocable motion. For now just sulk and slink away. Crushed.

* *

Bought the cheapest battery. Twelve-month guarantee. If they had one with a one-month guarantee, I would have bought it. Bought spark plugs. The cheapest. Pull away the tarp, raise the hood and connect the new life source and the eight receivers. Enter the driver's side and insert key. Pray to the gods of Detroit. The grinding noise proves the electrical system functions well enough. I can get turn over, but no ignition.

Gasoline. Grab the five-gallon can and drive to the 7-11. I'll treat my metal witch to premium unleaded. Pour most of the can into the tank opening. Pour about a half a cup into the carburetor. Prime the pump. More noise from the starter engine. Depress the accelerator once to avoid flooding. Almost start. Almost start. Almost start. With a triumphant explosion of energy and smoke from the tail pipe the engine catches and roars. *It's alive. It's alive.* After revving it a few times, I exit and let the beast idle. The thoughts of the early afternoon fill the void created by this accomplishment.

Under the hood. Wires, OK. Connectors, OK. Clamps, OK. Tubes, OK. Drain radiator and replace coolant/antifreeze tomorrow. Change oil, oil filter later, and air filter tomorrow. Add carburetor cleaner and fuel booster tomorrow. Put on four used tires tomorrow. Let engine run. I'm hungry.

Inside the cabin the food is scarce. Two jars of beans and frozen rolls. A six pack of Rolling Rock. What more could a man want? My guns. In the chest by the stone fireplace beneath the wood and a blanket is the lock box. 4-8-5-2 and lifts the lid to reveal two 9mm Glocks. The big boys. Fourteen in the clip and one in the pipe for fifteen missiles of destruction and death. Two boxes of cartridges. The guns are clean and ready for action. Eat before target practice.

Each squeeze of the trigger. Each report. Each recoil of the mechanism. Each bounce of the hand and arm. Each slam of the earth behind the tin cans. My dismay moves toward anger. After eighteen events, my anger has crescendoed. Fifteen events will allow the anger to subside and dissipate entirely. Night is about to wrap her arms around me. Time to go home.

* *

Television, my constant evening companion tells me about the trivial lives of two lesbians and their straight, naïve, roommate in Chicago, and the travails of an advertising exec, who chucks it all, moves to Montana and tries to become a cattle rancher. The other offerings are no better. Thank God for the movies on cable: multiple repeats of Grade B movies featuring people, who are now famous. The faux reality on TV is overwhelming. Time passes with the speed of an ice flow in February. The car lights through the kitchen window announce confrontation to come.

"Hey, you're up. That's nice. I had a hectic shift. So, I want to shower. Then let's have a drink. Or, are you way ahead of me."

"Nope, saving the best for you and the end of the day."

"I'll be right out."

The shower's sound is brief. I pour the drinks. Ellie appears in her light blue robe. Her hair is turbaned with a matching blue towel . . . ensemble du noir. I hand her a drink and she plops near the fire.

"That's better. This will make it even mo' better. How was your day, sweetie?"

She hoists her drink tome in a toast of companionship.

"Interesting. I got the old junker to start. Have to buy auto necessities tomorrow to complete its resurrection. But, it will fill the bill. The guns are in fine working order. Omar called about the ID's. Said his cousin could fix us up. We need to get him driver's license like photos by Tuesday. The six of us will take the pictures here tomorrow at ten, Omar will have them developed, and we can ship everything off to LA Monday. The cousin needs half up front. I have the money for us, but have to lend Tommy some cash. Oh, yeah, and I saw you going down on Jonteil. Upstairs on our bed. And, how was your day?"

I lifted my glass in a mock toast and took a long emphatic drink. The crackling of the wood sounded like the reports of the Glocks. My eyes were on her like two lasers; red beams of comprised of confusion, betrayal and anger.

"You were spying on me?"

"No. I came home to pick up the cabin key, which we keep in the kitchen. Remember. Saw Jonteil's car, knew she had been clothes' shopping, and thought she stopped by to display her purchases. Heard the music from up stairs and went to see. I saw just fine. Not fine. Not good. Not for me. How long has this been going on? Is she your lover? Where does this leave me? Us? Does Omar know? When were you going to tell me? Were you planning to leave me after our visit to Minneapolis? Maybe when you were there to scout out the distribution, you were going to arrange for my disappearance. For Omar's disappearance. Then you and Jonteil would be free to be with each other. What the fuck is happening?"

"Slow down. Let me tell you. Fix me another drink, will you? And one for yourself. You're trembling."

When I return to the couch, Ellie has pulled some pillows in front of the fireplace and is resting comfortably like in a shrink's office. Except her robe has opened to reveal more than the doctor would allow.

"Jonteil and I discovered each other about three months ago after one of the aerobic sessions. We were the last of the class to be in the showers. Our systems were pumping and the hormones were flowing. I took a long look at Jonteil's incredible sleek black body and knew I wanted to experience it. I never had feelings that strong for another women before. Men yes. Women no. I approached her, and she responded in kind. It was deliciously exciting. Since then we've wrestled with who we are and how we are living. Are we gay or bi-sexual? Could we live a dual life or only a singular one? We've had long talks about you and Omar. He has no earthly idea. How would you take it if we came out? Could you both accept who we are? Could you share us, if we wanted that? Could you bid us fond adieu, if that's what we wanted?

Each time we are together, we get deeper into a new life. Many times we don't have sex. We talk and just hang out. Aerobics, shopping, lunches, and drinks after my shift. But, I have to admit the sex is great. We even talked about asking you guys if you'd like to join us. Just talk about it. I admit I am selfish, but I'm not ready to share you with her and vice versa. Jonteil really feels the same. She has had only one other lesbian lover. Someone she knew at community college. The affair lasted only a semester.

Then came her depression and failing grades. She knew Omar as a friend of her brother from high school. They talked, but she never told him everything. Omar helped her recover psychologically, academically and sexually. So the sum and substance of Jonteil and me and you is that I don't know. Again, selfishly, I am content to continue leading two lives. I care deeply about both you and Jonteil. I care even deeper about my happiness. I like my life and I like who I am . . . for now. The question is can you live with it?"

"You are so full of half truths and shit, your skin is brown. Selfish is an inadequate word to describe your attitude and behavior. You would like to lead two lives. What about me? Let's see. You poke me in the eye and then tell me you're happy with your actions. Well, I'm not happy. How soon before Omar knows? I don't want to be the one to tell him, but he should know about his wife's life. Or, was Jonteil planning to keep that a secret forever?"

"I'll tell her that you know and suggest that she tell Omar. I ask that you bear with me, or us, and not mention a thing to him. I'm sorry you had to learn the way you did. It must have been devastating."

"No shit devastating. There was a part of me that wanted to join in. I mean, two beautiful women, sleek of form and hot of soul, with me between them. God, that's every boy's dream. But, that small part was drowned by betrayal. I was and am very confused and hurt. You know I care about you. Or, at least the you I thought I knew. Hell, I've even considered marriage. Glad I found out before I made a complete fool of myself.

Time is what all of us need. You and Jonteil have got to figure out who you want to be. I need time to figure what I'm going to do given the new circumstances. Omar will need time. Most important, we can't let anything interfere with the activities of the next few weeks. The success of our endeavors depends on teamwork. Teams are not derisive or destructive, which your actions are. So, you and Jonteil better calm down and rejoin the group. I'm going to bed. Wait; let's start now. Who gets the bed?"

"We do. You and me. No couch slumber for either one of us. As I said, I'm selfish and I like you and your body next to me for comfort and security. So, let's finish these drinks and go to our bed."

The flames from the logs are much shorter and subdued. Embers are becoming the dominant visual element around the andirons. The emotional peak and my lack of dinner have allowed the booze to work powerful magic. Ellie looks tempting on the floor. Anger, my shield, is deteriorating.

"Bric, sweetie, come sit with me. I need a hug and I know you need one, too."

As I slide from the couch, I realize how hard the booze has hit me. I stare at Ellie. Her robe is now open above and below the waist. Cinched by the Terri belt. She is bald. Her nipples peak out from beneath the fabric. I sit akimbo before this love temple. Once known and now new. She reaches to my neck and pulls my face to hers. The kiss is warmer and wetter than I can recall, as if I can recall anything. Gradually, my resistance and the robe are gone and I slide onto her.

"Make love to me. Be tender. Be strong. Do what ever you want with me. Just love me tonight."

Thus, commences an orgiastic frenzy of emotional contortions. I am wild with lust and anger. I must show her what she will miss, if she leaves me. I try to punish her with pleasurable pain for her indiscretion. More discomfort than she has ever enjoyed from me. She is not passive. Squeezing and tugging my flesh. Manipulating me and my face for her enjoyment. Legs in the air. Rump raised for acceptance of my mastery. Rug burn will be her badge of the evening's gratification. Hoarse breathing and whimpers fill the room. Pillows are tossed aside. The apex and the collapse are mutual. We embrace as she and Jonteil did earlier that day. The remnants of passion move aside for closure. Upstairs to a comfortable sleeping spot.

* *

I am awakened by the sound of car horns. Damn, it's 10:15. I'm alone in bed.

"Ellie?"

"In the kitchen getting coffee for both of us, while our friends gawk at me through the kitchen window. Assholes."

There is happiness in her voice. Giddiness I haven't heard for a long time. Then I see why. She is naked. She tried to sneak around the house and was caught red handed as it were.

"I'll throw on my pants and let the party animals in. They can find the coffee and whatever they want in the kitchen. Omar can prep the shot, while we get dressed and presentable for our immortal new images."

"Hey, Bric, do you guys always roam your ranch in the buff?"

"Nice shot of the woodland creature."

"Boys, settle down. Ellie, did you make enough coffee for all of us? Is there anything to eat? Omar kept me up all night or was that vice versa. I'm starved."

"Marilee and I stopped by the Union Street Bakery and picked up some fresh made honey buns and bear claws. Enough fat, sugar and carbos to keep us going all day."

"I'll be back in a jiffy. Need to shower and shave for my photo op. Help yourself to whatever. Omar, arrange the drapes to give a smooth background. Laundry clips are in the laundry. That's unique."

I was giddy with the pre-op phase. But crushed by what I learned last night. Still have to think about whom I am in Ellie's life and if she has a role in mine.

"Honey, I rinsed my hair and left the shower on for you."

"Thanks."

The water was screaming hot. Obviously she spiked it for me. She loves cool showers. Body wash serves as shampoo and shave cream. The latter only when I am covered with lather and have my eyes closed. Not sure why I shave with my eyes closed, but I've been doing it for years. I hear the shower door open and feel the coolness of new air.

"Ellie, what's going on"?

"More like who's getting off. Showers turn me on. Showers really turn me on. I want to show you how much."

Touching leads to kneading leads to stroking leads to kissing leads to full enclosure leads to rhythmic inhalation leads to shuddering completion. I am done with and in my shower. As I rinse, Ellie steps out and dries off. I wonder if this is how she approached Jonteil. I suffer a flash of post-coital depression.

"What have you two been doing up there so long?"

"Well, we wanted to be perfectly beautiful for our new life."

"Omar, are you ready for us?"

He will take test shots of the four so he could adjust the lens, background, and lighting. He is happy with the set. First Ellie than I stepped in front of the camera. In sixty seconds we knew what we had to do better for the real shot. The master took four shots of each of us and I took his four.

"I need to take the film card home for printing. Can't break down the set until after we have seen the results of this morning. Let's plan to meet back here at two."

"Can we make it at one. I need to get stuff for the car, which I can do before one and work on the car in the afternoon."

"One it is then. Jonteil, what are your plans?"

"I'll just hang here until you return. Hell that's less than two hours from now."

"Marilee and Tommy, what about you guys?"

"I'll stay for the hen party."

"I'll go with Bric to pick up the car stuff. I know he'll need me to help him work on the car and the Rolling Rocks later today. And we have to file the numbers off the three guns. When we dump them, no one should be able to trace them."

* *

Hen party, my ass. More like dyke revelry. I wonder if Marilee knows. I wonder if she is one of them. Tommy and I have to go to three different auto stores to avoid arousing suspicion. Paranoia prevents overconfidence. Overconfidence always leads to mistakes. The tires and the rest of the booty are in the trunk. The lid closes with some effort. Again, paranoia requires that no one observe what we have purchased. An open trunk lid would be a red flag. I slip Tommy the cash he is missing. Back home by one-ten.

Omar is so damned proud of himself he wants to dance. He has succeeded is replicating the driver's license ID photos . . . angle, distance, background and the non posed stupid look. Jonteil collects the shots and cash. She will take care of the overnight mailing on Monday.

Marilee wants to shop . . . food and clothes. Ellie complains of a brutal week and will take a well-deserved nap. Jonteil and Omar head for places unknown. She looks resigned to her fate. Tommy and I set out for an afternoon of car and gun work.

BLUE MONDAY

The alarm greets the new day with discordant promise. From sheets to shower and store in less than forty minutes, excited about what we have done and what we have to do this week. More details and more questions. Big job is to lock-in itineraries. I plan, but every one has to buy his or her own tickets . . . preferably one person at a time. Jonteil comes into my office and closes the door.

"We have to talk."

"No more dialin' and sneerin'. That part of business is over. Hell the business is over."

"Not about business. We have to talk about . . . you know."

"Yes, I know. And there is not much new light you can shed on the situation. How did things go with Omar?"

"He's crushed. I am afraid he may do something drastic or stupid."

"You mean like leave you or hurt you out of anger."

"No. Something else that might screw up what the six of us need to accomplish."

"Let me tell you right now, if what you and Ellie have together causes your husband to fuck up the operation, I will blame the pair of you. It's your responsibility to make sure your husband holds up his end of the bargain. He has certain things that are his responsibility . . . family connections we don't have. Connections, which are vital to the success of our efforts. So far he has delivered. Don't stop him now by the affair of your love-in. You must do whatever is necessary to keep him together. Keep him focused. Keep him as part of the team. The job is more important than all of us and certainly anyone of us. Our reward is directly the result of all individual efforts."

"He didn't speak to me all Sunday. He drank a lot, went to bed, and locked the bedroom door. He was gone before I got up this morning. Could you talk to him?"

"What would you like me to say? Should I tell him it's OK that his wife and my lover share each other's bodies and souls from time to time? It's OK that he shares his wife with my lover? Gee, Omar, I think it's just great that Ellie can get off on Jonteil. I just love sharing my most intimate moments with another . . . and most particularly when that that other is a woman. You should feel great that Jonteil can do the same. Omar, dear buddy, my masculinity has not been shaken, why should yours be in jeopardy? Maybe Black men take this sort of thing more deeply than their poor white cousins. You know penis size and all that crap.

Or, should I suggest that the four of us get together for a group grope? Or, maybe just Omar and I for a little one-on-one like basketball at the Y. No and fuck you. I will not talk to Omar to smooth over the eruption you have caused. I will not be the peacemaker to your war. That is your job as an adult and as his wife. But, I will talk to Omar as part of my role as team leader. Talk business, all business. Very objective and seemingly unaffected by the recent events including your confessions. Do you understand my position?"

"I was hoping you could try to explain how you felt and how you reacted. Maybe if he saw this he would be more understanding."

"I do appreciate your inconsiderate invitation to reopen the wound in my soul and fill it with Iodine, but I must regretfully decline. More understanding? I understand that Ellie and you have a thing going on and it's been going on for a few months. I understand that the relationship between Ellie and me is, for all intents and purposes, on the rocks. I understand that I most likely will have to walk away from that relationship or watch Ellie walk away. I understand that I am in great emotional turmoil. I suspect Omar is suffering the same. Ellie and I will resolve our relationship. I suggest you and Omar do the same. And do it quickly. Now, I have work to do, and so do you."

KAYAK gives me all sorts of options to fly the six of us from Duluth to Albuquerque using multiple interim destinations. We will all meet and stay at the Thunderbird Motel on I-40. To make the transformation from robber to drug dealer complete, I'll have to know the names on the cards we are purchasing from Omar's cousin. He arrives by car, then meets me. I sign my cards and get them laminated before we check into the Thunderbird. As each person arrives, the procedure will be repeated so that when we check into the motel we will have different identities than when we stepped off the plane. All old identifications and wallet stuffing must be destroyed completely. Burned. The transformation must be complete. Omar must get me all the new names in the next few days.

Ellie is going to the Twin Cities tomorrow. Her roommate from nursing school. A surprise visit from a friend. Ellie says her old roommate lives downtown in a luxury high rise. If she deals, the authorities can't suspect anything. She is the Senior Administrator in the city's largest hospital. Plus, she comes from a wealthy family. She has always had money. I wonder how close the two were in Nursing School.

After the cash acquisition, we will dump the outfits and the guns in the trunk of the car I leave at the Twin Cities airport. Have to make sure all the VIN numbers are scraped off the car. No way to easily trace ownership. We need time. Must wipe down the engine and the interior to remove fingerprints. Run the car through the wash twice to remove exterior prints. Call Omar and Tommy for a meeting at the cabin tonight. Make sure Omar knows what is really important . . . the job. His failed marriage must take a back seat.

* *

"Tommy, now that you're a man of leisure, do you plan to sleep all day."

"Up yours. I've got my shit together. Gloves, masks, coveralls, and already scraped the numbers off my dad's .38. Marilee wants to contribute. What can she do?"

"She'll be valuable on our return to the northland. She'll be a driver. For now, she just questions everything we do, like a consultant, and she gets to St. Louis."

"Cool. I got to say . . . we're ready."

"Tonight at my cabin, you, Omar and I must have one more walk through of details. Then the six of us will meet Wednesday or Thursday night at the cabin to make sure we have thought of everything. We'll need a practice run next weekend."

What time tonight?"

"Seven."

* *

Omar's voice sounds like a 45 played at 33 1/3. Depression and a hangover have killed his verve. He agrees to be there at seven. The rest of my day is spent as a cyber travel coordinator.

"Omar, Jesus, man you look like shit. What's wrong?"

"I'm ferociously hung over."

"Omar, I'll need the new names from your cousin so I can make reservations at the motel. I can send a money order to hold the rooms in our new names. How soon do you think your cousin can get us the names?"

"I think in two days. I'll call him."

"Also tell him that he must meet me at the airport so that I can change my identity before arriving at the motel. I'll make him a reservation under any name he wants. Tell him I'll have the balance of cash for all the cards when he meets me."

"Done."

"OK, I have everybody's itinerary here. Omar will fly to Tampa. He'll be met by Jonteil. They stay one night and fly to Albuquerque. Tommy, you go to Canada then to Dallas, stay one day then to our base. Marilee will fly to St. Louis. Stays two days and heads to the Big Q . . . hey not bad. Ellie flies to Denver with me for the ski trip. We drive to the Big Q in a one-way airport-to-airport rental . . . a sight seeing tour. Ellie and I arrive first. Sometime on the morning of T minus two. Two days before the buy. I meet Omar's cousin. Just what is his name anyway?"

"Ahmed."

"Great, I call Ahmed and he comes to the Albuquerque airport car rental spot. Ellie and I change personas, and pay him for the other four. Hopefully he has started to make contact. I don't want to sit around the motel for more than two days . . . three tops. All the team gets transitioned. We make the buy. Ahmed leaves with his grease, and we head back to the Twin Cities. One question: return trip. Should we drive back to the Twin Cities or should we fly back using the same type of circuitous routes we used before the sale? Any suggestions?"

"Let's drive back. It'll be less conspicuous."

"Yes, but more time consuming. What if the police get lucky, and are waiting for us?"

"No police force is that good. We will be out of New Mexico, back to the Twin Cities, and far away before the dummies find the junker. Besides, the drive back is not more than two long days."

"My cousin can probably get us cars . . . for a price."

"Jesus, by the time he is paid, he'll be an equal partner. We'll get the cars ourselves. We'll buy the cutting powder and small plastic bags and everything else we need in the Q. And, I don't want him to buy guns there. He should bring them with him from LA. That means he'll have to drive from LA. For what we're paying him, a little road time should not be an inconvenience. The purchase of three pieces could be discovered by our new business associates. I don't want our drug suppliers to get worried or feel threatened that we are carrying in advance of the meeting. Let them assume we're just squareheads from the Midwest. Guys who want no hassle. Just a clean transaction."

"Bric, I think we should drive back to the Twin Cities. We don't want authorities to have any clue about us. How, where, and when we were reborn. We'll buy cars from some sleazy used car dealer with our phony ID's. Pay cash. If the local cops get an itch they'll scratch it back to LA. We should buy an SUV or something that holds six. Or, are maybe two cars better. Maybe we can even leave them next to the junker we use to acquire our seed money. How about that for irony?"

"Right, Tommy. We'll drive back east in two cars. Before we get to the Twin Cities, we'll need a place where we can cut and package the shit. Some fleabag motel. I'll figure that out. What about license plates? The New Mexico plates will invite curious eyes."

"I can get temporary Minnesota tags from my pal at the Superior Motors. Three off the bottom of the pack. One for the junker and two for the return cars. I'll pack them away and we can tape them on the rear windows after we're out of New Mexico."

"We'll have less than a day to cut, repackage, and sell. Ellie will have to contact the dealer as we approach Minneapolis. We have to allow time for the dealer to contact Ellie's friend. Shit, I'll bet she'll want something for her introduction. That will be Ellie's job to find out. Now, we can't be too early, or word will leak out and the junkies will start a pre-feeding frenzy of rumors. They'll tell all their buddies that they're going to be well, because so-and-so is getting a shipment. The cops will hear of the shipment and we'll waltz into a trap. Timing is everything . . . from top to bottom . . . from beginning to end."

"After the final deal, I think Marilee and I will just disappear. You know, hide in plain sight. She's thinkin' Florida. Some place like Sarasota, Venice or Fort Myers. We'll be just another couple who fled the hurly-burly of Los Angeles for the laid-back life of West Coast of the Sunshine State. We can take menial jobs, build a decent rep, and in a few years maybe open our own store or something. We'll be just two of the thousands of immigrants, who slide under the radar screen into Florida each year, and we're not even Spanish."

"Have you figured out how you would get to Florida? Fly or drive?"

"We'll fly part way and drive the rest just to muddy our tracks. We'll have to buy a car, say in Nashville, but it will be fine. A new start. Omar, what about you and Jonteil?"

"We don't know yet. I like the idea of flying to an island that requires no passport. Then island hopping until we reach a place where no one cares who we are or what we might have done. I have a few places in mind, but nothing concrete yet. I think that's what Jonteil wants to do, but I'm not 100% sure. Bric?"

"Ellie wants to go south and I want to stay north. So we'll probably go west. Small town off the path. We'll need to invent details of our new personas. Maybe I'll be a writer of twisted adult fiction and Ellie will be my sex-slave. Maybe vice versa. She and I will have to work on that soon. OK. Before we leave tonight, Omar please inspect the three guns to make sure we have completely scraped off all the serial numbers. A fresh pair of eyes is always a good idea. We will need to wipe down all part that we may have been touched. Get rid of all prints. I'll wash the chariot of the gods at the *Fuel N Foam* next week. One last item, the six of us should meet for a planning and details session Thursday. Here, away from the eyes and ears of neighbors. Is seven OK?"

Ellie is excited about her trip to Minneapolis. Sharon lives the good life. Works hard. Plays hard. Rests in luxury. After she was caught with her hand in the family business cash register, her folks cut her off, but the rest of the world has no idea. She keeps a good public face. Educated woman, socially acceptable, with a high level visible job. The drug trade filled her life with money to replace her inheritance and her bed with attractive young men. She was a queen not a toy.

The recent sweep by the state and federal DEA eliminated a lot of competition. She went back to selling prescription medications on a very lucrative, but temporary basis. Her scheme is simple. She does the hospital inventory, places the order, and skims from the delivery. The hospital orders and receives a specific quantity. The drug detailer delivers the "extra" to her home, and receives compensation for the overage. Sometimes all cash, sometimes a mix of cash, drugs, and pleasure.

Sharon is interested in buying whatever we can deliver. She is willing to pay a small premium for some pre-package smack, and fair market price for the uncut shit. It makes the entire deal clean. There will be no mess in her apartment and no payment for someone to do the processing. Plus, it's then easy for her street contacts to move the shit quickly. She'll pay between 50-60 per gram, depending on quality. Ellie told her she would have six kees. And would be contacting her in two or three weeks.

* *

Omar calls. It's 10:30.

"What's going on?"

"By now you must have realized that Jonteil told me all about her and Ellie. Needless to say I'm destroyed. I had no idea. I mean sex between us seemed to be getting better and better. I now know why. Her true sexual component was awakening. I was just there. She told me that Ellie told you. I need some guidance here. How did you handle her telling you? What did you say?"

"First, Ellie didn't tell me. I came upon the two of them exploring each other on my bed. They never saw me. I confronted Ellie that night. Second, the whole thing came as a real shock to me. I mean it put a huge crimp in any family plans I might have been making. Third, I have swept it away. Whatever happened or will happen between the two of them as well as Ellie and me cannot interfere with our present project. The work comes first. When we are done . . . in less than two weeks, Ellie and I will sort out our lives. I suggest that you and Jonteil adopt the same approach. If the two of them want to head off into the sunset, so be it. I will start anew. I'll find someone new."

"How can you be so cold?"

"Cold my ass. Pragmatic. Objective. Those are better descriptions of my attitude. This thing we are about to do is bigger than anything we have ever attempted. We have the chance for a giant, all-inclusive do over. And nobody's sexual proclivity is going to fuck that up. I am appropriately prioritizing. Big head first."

"How can you just ignore the betrayal?"

"I'm not ignoring it. I'm putting into its proper perspective given what we must accomplish in the next two weeks. Besides, Ellie is not my flesh and blood. She is an adult with whom I have had a very pleasing relationship for the past few years. I had relationships with others before and will have them with others after. Was Jonteil the first and only woman you slept with and loved? Not likely. For you, also, there will be others. How you resolve your penis problems is your call. You have to be prepared to walk away from Jonteil as you would a favorite pet, which ran away.

You are entitled to be sad and pissed. You are entitled to feel betrayed. But, you are not entitled to let your feelings get in the way of your work. Take what happened seriously, just not personally. There will be lots of time for self-indulgent pity and recriminations after we complete our mission. Until then, direct your anger toward Jonteil sexually. Do stuff to her and with her you've seen in movies or dreamed about. Enjoy your newfound sexual freedom. But, stay focused on the job at hand."

I think this is not what Omar wanted me to say. He wanted me to express pity or some other contrived emotion. But, he got my truth and he knows it. He also knows I'll be strong for him after the deal is done. I'll be strong for all of the others, just as they will be strong for me. Talk through tomorrow night, after Ellie gets home from her shift.

"We must buy airline tickets tomorrow. I'll make motel reservations and send a money order confirming the rooms after Ahmed gets me my new name. Must have by Thursday"

"OK."

* *

One final meeting of the team to triple-check the details from every angle.

"I have the disguises, pepper spray, and three guns properly prepared. I'll put them in the trunk of the car until we need them."

"Tommy, if you go to the garage, you'll find the bags from L.L. Bean. We'll need to pack them as far in advance as possible, but save room for the cash."

"Has everybody made excuses at work for the time off? No more than one week. Omar and Jonteil will leave together. Be visible. Marilee, you head out of town on Sunday. Ellie, you leave Tuesday morning, first thing. We'll meet in Albuquerque. I'll be there before you guys arrive. We will make the buy the next day, and leave for Minneapolis the day after that or maybe that night. Drive straight through. Arrive in the Twin Cities in two long days. I will make reservations at some place near the warehouse district. We'll contact Ellie's friend when we have the prepared merchandise for sale. The night we arrive or next day. After the sale we divvy up the proceeds, square accounts, and go our separate ways. Now the details of the first day."

"About three on Tuesday we arrive around the corner from the bank's back entrance dressed in everything except the masks. If all goes according to schedule, the truck will arrive between 3:15 and 3:30. As it pulls up we'll run to the side and force entry as one guard is opening to door and before he can press the button to alert the guard inside that the unloading process can begin. I figure from the time the guard opens the door until we have relieved the truck of the cash bags; we have no more than two minutes. Hopefully less. We hit both guards with pepper spray and wrap their faces, hands, and feet with duct tape. I can spray through the driver's door and Tommy, you, can spray the driver from the opening between the cab and the box. The guns are not to be used. They are just for show. Just to let the two jamokes know we are serious."

"Bric, suppose the guard behind the wheel gets brave and pulls his gun?"

"I'll hit him, before I shoot him. If the entire deal falls on its ass, we are likely to be treated with consideration if no one is shot. If one of the guards is shot, and we don't escape, we'll face twenty-five to life. So, no shooting unless shot at. Jonteil?"

"The multiple car accident will happen at 3:05 at Six Corners, beyond the mall. It should draw a big crowd and numerous police, fire, and rescue vehicles. Fortunately, Ellie and I will be OK. A lot of damage to our car. Not us. I'll have the police take me home. From there Omar and I will catch the airborne stage out of town. The same cop will probably take Ellie home. She can drive her car to the airport that evening to catch her flight to Denver, meeting you in Minneapolis. After the robbery, what will you do with the cash?"

"We'll go through all the bags and pull out only twenties and larger. The change, singles, and checks will be left. We'll dump the cash into our three bags and lock them for air transportation. All of our paraphernalia will be ditched in the trunk of the car. We keep the gloves on until we each exit the car. There will be no prints. I take Tommy to the seaplane and Omar to his home. I head to Minneapolis airport for my evening flight to Denver. I meet Ellie at the airport. After one night in Denver, we drive to the Big Q, where we will meet with you guys as you deplane from your intermediate points."

"We all have alibis and return flights. What are we missing?"

"Cash."

"Yeah, everybody should have some of their own cash. Leave some in the bank so it looks like you'll be back from your trip. But, take as much as you can. Big bills. No travelers' checks. No credit cards at all. All present and soon-to-be-former identification will be confiscated by me and destroyed. Keep nothing of your past. Hell, buy new clothes in Albuquerque. We'll throw away all the stuff that we brought from Duluth. Keep no pictures, notes, or letters from anybody. Your past must disappear."

"When should we rehearse?"

"We'll have a drive through on Saturday. We'll meet here at two, go to our appointed spots, and make our rounds. Each car will keep a log of time and note any things, which could cause problems on Tuesday. Tomorrow I'll to go to the cabin and visit the car one last time. Fill it with gasoline and drive it for about an hour. Can't afford a breakdown on the Interstate to the Twin Cities. OK. See you guys on Saturday."

The partners in crime leave. Omar still looks forlorn. Marilee was quiet all evening. Hope she isn't getting cold feet. Better call Tommy tomorrow to make sure he keeps her in line. Ellie showers and slithers between the sheets as I fake slumber.

* *

"Bric, did you talk to Omar yesterday?"

"Yes, and I'll be damned if I'm going to get caught up in some silly game of high school he-said-she-said."

"I'm curious what you told him?"

"Basically, what I told you. Keep your dirty linen out of the way of the job at hand. We have serious work and if we are distracted by affairs of the heart, our work will suffer. And if he fucks up and our project suffers for it, I'll wreak havoc on both Omar and his estranged wife. Your issues are your issues and can be resolved after Minneapolis. OK."

"That's it?"

"Yes. Why?"

"No real reason. Thanks. I think we can sit on our issues until after the deal is done."

"That's nice."

* *

The deadbeats, whose names appeared in the newspaper and in our letters to the business community groups, threaten me with lawsuits and violence. In two weeks, they'll just have to find me if they want to kick my ass. Thursday night. Think I'll treat Ellie to dinner at the Marriott. Reach her at the nurses' station. A couple enjoying an evening meal . . . our Last Supper. No conversation about the future only the present and the past.

Shrove Tuesday

I am up twenty minutes before the alarm can herald the day. I am prepped, primed, and pumped. The event, departure, convening, and the second event are firm. There will be no deviation or slip up of a personal nature. The plan and its participants are tight with all the details and the timing. In eight hours I will be on an irrevocable course to a new life. A real do over. Ellie does not stir when I leave the bed for the kitchen. Coffee cupped, it's back upstairs to cleanse my costume of flesh. She does not move as I dress. Soon it will be time for her to rise for her part in the theatre du jour.

Sipping my wake-up potion, I wander the house. The place that has been my home for years. The place to which I will not return. I am leaving more than physical remnants of my life; I am leaving laughter, fear, anger, and love. All my emotions are imbedded in the walls and the furniture. They will be the sounds of ghosts for the next tenants. I see all the chores I thought I should do, but never got around to. I see all the minor fixes, which should have been made. I sense the potential alterations, which we were going to make if we bought the place. All these things, real and imagined, are no longer important. It's important that we act with resolution and precision. And that we stick to the plan.

"Bric, are you here?"

"Yep, downstairs. Do you want your coffee now?"

"What time is it?"

"8:35."

"OK, coffee would be nice."

Her favorite mug. Honey, milk and coffee. Upstairs. She is in the fetal position. Normally she is spread-eagled, taking up her space and a portion of mine. Powerful under-currents of fear of the unknown have caused her body to curl into a protective posture. She knows that I will not hurt her. I don't think she knows I am concerned about the upcoming events.

I have never let any of them know just how concerned I am. The size of the opportunity dictates the size of concern. I don't think she knows how deeply she has hurt me, or how I have buried that hurt for the cause. The little boy part of me wants to slip under the single sheet that contours the details of her naked body so that I can enjoy a momentary release of tension. The grown up knows that tension now is good because it keeps me focused.

"Up an at 'em sleepy head. Coffee is here to nourish your neurons."

"Thanks, sweetie. Why don't you get out of those clothes and be with me?"

"Thanks, sweetie. But, we have much last minute checking to do and not much time to do it. There'll be time for us tonight in Denver."

* *

I bound out the bedroom door as she plods to the bathroom. Omar and Tommy are due at ten. After we pick up the clunker, we'll drive Tommy's car back to his place. Omar's car will never leave home today.

"Hey guys, coffee is in the kitchen. Help yourself."

"Omar, any last minute conversations with Ahmed?"

"Yesterday he confirmed he is arriving in the Big Q about six hours before you arrive at the airport. He'll check into the Thunderbird under the agreed-to name of Dewey Cheetum. He is driving an Infinity 45Q. Chocolate black. He will have all the necessary items. Before you arrive he will confirm contact with the sellers and layout a place for the transaction. Then he will meet you at the airport."

"I hope you told him I want the deal to go down in an open place with a lot of public access. I don't want to be ambushed by the dealers, and I'm sure they don't want to be ambushed by me. And that I want the deal to be complete within forty-eight hours of our arrival."

"He knows all that. He also said he was bringing a guest . . . a traveling companion. He never leaves home without one. He may stay a few extra days in the Big Q to clear his mind and soul. I suspect this traveling companion is not only his ho, but also his body guard."

"Whatever he wants to do is fine with me so long as it does not interfere with the deal."

"Ahmed did want to know how many kees we would be buying. Knowing the amount would make his dealings with the Mexicans that much faster. I said that would depend on the amount of capital we were able to acquire. I told him you would call the motel and leave a message for his arrival."

"Good."

"Tommy, is our battle gear ready."

"In the trunk of my car. The gloves I got were extra long at the wrists so we could pull them up over the sleeves of the jump suits. No flesh will be visible. That's important for Omar. The suits are bright orange. The perfect color for the red hair on the clown masks. I got us used sneakers so we can dump everything external when we are done. Plus, and here is the best part, I personally tested the three cans of pepper spray. They work good. A one or two second spray blinded me for about a minute. So, I figure that when we spray the guards, we should really dose them. About five seconds of spray in each eye should make them useless as witnesses."

"Jesus, Tommy, that's over the edge, even for you. I would have trusted the instructions. But, it's good to know the shit works. We're done here. Let's go to the cabin and wait. Ellie, we're heading out now."

"Bric, can you come up here for a second."

"I'll be with you guys real quick."

"Ellie?"

"In the bathroom."

The steam is roiling from the doorway. She is standing at the shower. Her hair is tangled from the first attempt at drying. No other towel in sight.

"I need a big hug. I'm real nervous."

The hug is genuine, but there is a strong indication that Ellie wants more. I break off.

"You'll be fine. Just do what we discussed. Have the accident. Get home. Get to the airport and meet me in Minneapolis on our way to Denver."

"Can't you stay and be here for me?"

"Not bloody likely. I have work to do. I cannot be distracted. See you on the plane."

* *

My shirt and pants are wet from Ellie's body. No matter. We drive to the cabin. Then take Tommy's car home. The three of us wait like we're in free fall. As the old joke goes, *It's not the fall that hurts; it's that damned sudden stop.* There are twenty-four hours in each 60 minutes we wait. At two-fifteen we dress and clear away any reminder of our presence. Jumpsuits, sneakers, and gloves are on when we enter the car. We hold the guns and pepper spray cans in the masks on our laps.

Our parking spot awaits us next to the Dumpster in an entrance to the alley behind the bank. The same entrance to be used by the truck. I don't care if they see the old car, just not the people in it. It is now 2:54. We wait in silence. By now Jonteil and Ellie are approaching their destination.

Every time I glance at my watch, I note the excruciating passage of less than one minute. I try not to think of the two decoys as my lover and her lover. I think of the decoys as inanimate objects set out to complete a task. Tommy and Omar have not moved. I can see sweat on both faces.

"Tommy, what's your job when the truck arrives?"

"I run up to the side door before it opens. When the guard opens the door and before he can secure it to the bank wall, I grab him and spray him good. Then I hook the door to the wall, and enter the compartment with the cash bags."

"Omar?"

"I am right behind Tommy and take the bags from him as he unloads. We unload until the truck is empty, placing every bag in the car's trunk."

"And you, Bric?"

"I run to the driver's door and try to open the door. Failing that, I brandish my gun in a way that demands he open it. If he fails to do that immediately, I hit the truck side and Tommy fills the cab with pepper spray from the back, while I do the same from the air hole in the door. The trick is to incapacitate the driver before he can use the radio to alert the bank. I figure I have three seconds before he tries to call for help. So, be alert in the back, Tommy. Everybody OK?"

"It's 3:10. Masks on."

"Bric, can you help pull this damned thing down under the collar. I'll do the same for you and then get Tommy. I never though I'd be happy to be a white clown."

"Silence. From here on there is no talking."

More waiting. The heat inside the mask is nearly stifling. I check Tommy and Omar. They're identities are completely hidden. More waiting. With the full body disguise, I can't raise my sleeve to be tortured by my watch. I can't allow myself the luxury of thinking about what I will do with my share. Stay focused.

Around the corner lumbers the cash tank. As it passes the car, the three of us exit. We run directly behind the truck, hugging the back door, out of range of the rear view mirrors. Brake lights tell us we are at ground zero. Tommy moves to the right side of the vehicle, and Omar to the right rear corner. The squealing of brakes foretells the stop. We are go.

I don't hear the activity on Tommy's side. I grab the driver side door handle as the door opens. The driver violated some rule and was getting out for a smoke. The last thing he saw was a clown spraying his eyes.

"Shit, what the fuck is going on? That hurts. Fuck I can't see. Who are you? What do you want? What's going on?"

His jabbering questions go unanswered. He tries to reach for his gun and rub his eyes at the same time. His staggering and flailing warrant a brutal smack on the side of the head.

He falls. I tape his eyes, mouth, and hands. Then, push his overweight flopping body beneath the truck. I glance at Omar as he heads to the car with several bags in each hand. He raises the trunk lid and dumps his load. I hurry to the open side door, grab a few bags, and sprint for the car. On my return, I pass Omar with two big bags.

The pops of the gun go almost unnoticed because of our masks and scampering. When I return to the open door, I see the guard on the floor. He has three holes in his head. One in the nose and one in each eye socket. A red pool has formed beneath his head. His hands and feet are twitching. Then there is no other movement. Unmasked, Tommy hands me four very full bags and he grabs the last two of the large bags. Other than the dead guard, the truck is empty. Omar and I retrieve the guard from under the truck and toss him in with his partner. We slam the door and run back to the car. Masks removed, we deliberately head for the parking lot by the auditorium. Cannot speed or be noticed. Silence.

"I had no choice. When I sprayed him I think I missed. He kept coming at me and pulled my mask off. He recognized me. Even called me by name. I had no choice. I'm sorry.

"It just puts the remains of the day under a tighter microscope. We can't undo what has been done. Let's open the bags and divide the money. I figure it'll be fifteen minutes before anyone notices the truck and goes to investigate. It'll be another ten minutes before the cops arrive. We have twenty-five minutes to get the cash ready for flight. So, let's go."

Bag by bag the loot is removed and placed equally into our three pieces of securable luggage. The small stuff and extraneous paperwork are left in the bank bags, which are dumped in the trunk. There is one hell of a lot of money. The last bags with *Nooners* logos are packed full.

"Looks like the saloon had a banner weekend. They even wrapped the stacks with their own bands, and noted the amount in each stack. How cute. One stack for Omar. One stack for Tommy. One stack for you, Bric. It's like dealing cards. One for me, one for you and one for you. Do you want the next round face up or face down?"

"Shit, take a look at those cards. Those are stacks of fifties. One hundred in a stack. That's five grand. Not fifty twenties per stack like the other bags. Fuck, there are stacks of hundreds. That's ten grand per stack. Where did they get this money? No saloon can have that good a weekend. Even a four-night drunk along. Tommy, open the other bag."

"Mother pus bucket. We hit another treasure chest. Twenties and fifties. And at least three more stacks of hundreds."

"Finish dividing, I'll count."

I remove the stacks from my bag as two more come from Omar in the backseat.

"I got a rough count of 130 grand per bag, maybe more. That's about 400 total. Omar, your cousin said twenty per kee, right. We can get between fifteen and twenty kees for sale in the Twin Cities. I'll leave him that message. We'll each take ten for travelling expenses. But, don't flash it. Just spend it as needed."

The three of us stare in disbelief. Our final compensation was going to be over one million and a half. Half million for each couple.

"OK, we got really lucky. Sort of galactic compensation for killing the guard. You know, good balances bad. Now put everything except our three bags in the trunk. Remember keep the gloves on until after you exit the car. Tommy, you're the first stop. Your plane leaves in forty minutes."

We drive down the peninsula with lake on one side and a marina on the other. The seaport is at the end. We drop Tommy a couple hundred yards from the seaport.

"Tommy, so far so great. Forget about the guard. He was a risk that you eliminated."

"Thanks, Bric. See you guys in the Big Q."

I make a U-turn and head for Omar's house. We have to go through downtown. There is a flurry of squad cars and EMS vehicles apparently heading for the bank.

"Hope Jonteil is safe. See you guys in a few days."

* *

The sun is bright and it warms the cool air that lingers. Large clumps of cinder-encrusted snow and ice are occasionally visible on the side of the interstate that runs from Duluth to Minneapolis. Eight miles out of town and the profile of my former hometown is no longer visible in the rear view mirror. Twenty miles out of town and I am centered on the failure of the acquisition. Why the hell did Tommy have to shoot? Did he really have to shoot? Was his mask pulled off at all or did Tommy just get antsy and pop the old guy?

The well-planned robbery is now a felony murder. We are all guilty of the murder, because we were all committing the underlying felony of grand larceny. One safety hatch has just been locked. Can't change the events. But, must be ready to make it right with the authorities if they catch up to us. Should Tommy be offered as a sacrificial lamb? After all, he fired the shot. How to get Tommy in front of the crime without anyone seeing me behind him? Work that through in my subconscious. Watch him closely for next few days. Can't afford another fuck up. Should he even have a gun? If not, he'll get worried about my motives. OK. Just keep him in plain sight. Where does all this leave Marilee? About ninety minutes and I be waiting in the airport.

"Midwest Distribution, good afternoon. How may I help you?"

"Ben Gustafson please."

"Gustafson. How may I help you?"

"Ben, it's me, Bric. How you doing?"

"Great, Bric."

"Nothing special. Listen I wanted to thank you for lunch today at the Oak Grille. The fish was terrific."

"Huh, oh yeah. I'm glad you enjoyed it. It was good to get the financial matters worked out. I know you know that you're one of our best customers and we look forward to a long a prosperous relationship."

"Want you to know how much I appreciate you guys working with me until I get my receivables reduced to a workable level. Let me know when you'll be up in Duluth so you can see what I've done with the cabin."

"Sure thing old buddy. Say, I got to run to a meeting. Call you soon. Bye."

My alibi. Lunch in Minneapolis with a wholesaler rep to review my over due account. A business meeting from 12:30 to 2:30. I could not have been in Duluth at the time of the robbery, murder. I know Ben will back me up. He's been taking cash from me for phony invoices for about two years. Best of all I have pictures of him and his toy playing swallow the weenie on the couch at the cabin. His wife of eighteen years would not approve. Airport twenty miles.

Long-term parking. Take ticket. Pull into a line of cars in one of the middle rows. No car came after my entrance and there is no activity in the cars around mine. My bag is in the back seat. Remove temp tag from rear deck. Hope the entry camera did not read it. Close and lock. Walk leisurely to the terminal. Toss key and paper tag down storm drain. No one in sight. United Airlines ticket counter.

* *

"May I help you?"

"Yes, I'm booked on your flight 1029 to Denver at seven-fifteen today. I'd like to check this."

"Has anyone given you anything to take on board the plan?"

"No."

"Has your bag been in your sight and care since you packed it?"

"Yes."

"Would you fill out one of the baggage tags while I process your ticket?"

"There you're all set Mr. Bricsonn. The flight leaves from Gate 34, Concourse D. Just take the escalator behind you to the second level and follow the signs to Concourse D. Have a nice flight. Will you be spring skiing?"

"No this is a relaxation trip."

In a series of fluid motions and vacuous conversation, the airline accepted my future and would transport the cash and its temporary owner away from a murder scene and state of confusion. I have time to get some coffee before Ellie arrives on the flight from Duluth.

"*The top story from your ActionTeam is the brazen daylight bank robbery and murder in Duluth. Three individuals dressed as clowns robbed an armored truck and killed one of the guards, who were bringing cash from local merchants to the Norst Bank in downtown Duluth. For an on scene exclusive report we go to Win Westerly. Win what more can you tell our viewers?*"

"*Well, Jennifer, details are sketchy, but here's what we've been able to piece together. At approximately 3:15 PM today, as the armored truck was unloading the weekend's deposits from numerous merchants, three individuals, we think they were men, dressed in bright orange jumpsuits and clown masks, set upon the truck. They pepper-sprayed the guards and took the bags of cash. One guard, 54-year-old Angelo Berlini, who was responsible for unloading the bags of money from the truck was shot and killed. The driver, 58-year-old Lars Olson, was bound with duct tape and left in the truck. Bank officials are unable to confirm how much money was in the bags. As you know this past weekend was the annual SpringFest. So, it is safe to assume that the robber's haul was substantial. The bank is contacting the merchants in an effort to determine exactly how much was taken.*"

"*Win, does anyone know any details about the robbers?*"

"*The only details we are able to report are those issued by the police relative to the clown costumes. The driver has been hospitalized for observation. The police will be questioning him shortly and they will release the details, so they say. Right now the officials are saying nothing. Jennifer, I'll stay here and report as we learn more. For ActionTeam News this is Win Westerly in Duluth.*"

They gotta big set for charging three dollars for a paper cup of coffee. They tell me the beans are grown in the sacred land of some obscure tribe in South America. I'm supposed to feel privileged to drink it. Well, I'm rich enough not to care about paying the three bucks. Time to shuffle to the gate.

In the hundreds of people going somewhere in a hurry, I search out Ellie. She will be more difficult to spot than Jonteil and Omar . . . a black couple in the land of whiteness.

"Jesus, what the hell happened to you? Are you all right?"

"My seat restraint gave too much and I hit the dash. The paramedics say there is no apparent bone damage. Just contusions and hemotoma. I'll have a shiner for a few days. But I can breathe through my nose and see fine from both eyes. Hell, I got banged up worse two years ago when we were riding the giant inner tubes on the hill out on Three Pine Road. Remember?"

"Yeah. It's just a shock, I guess. How is Jonteil?"

"She's fine. Her restraint held. She received a few body bruises. The paramedics said there was no reason for us to go to the ER. But, our doctors should see us, if the conditions become aggravated. The car was totaled."

"How did you guys pull off the accident?"

"We hung back from the stop sign on the side of the road. Traffic would ebb and flow. Jonteil noticed a delivery truck from your store . . . how's that for irony . . . coming from the left. As the truck approached the stop sign, she moved onto the road and accelerated. Just as the truck was in the intersection she slammed into the side panel. The car and truck spun out of control and slid into two other cars and some painter's truck. In about six seconds there was glass and pieces of exterior metal all over the intersection. We saw later that there were a few rear-enders, but no one was seriously hurt.

The cops came . . . local, county and state. We had them all plus both EMS trucks. We exchanged insurance cards and signed the accident report. The officer in charge told Jonteil there would have to be a hearing because of the amount of damage and the cause of reckless driving. The ticket alone was for $285. Jonteil will have to pay a hefty fine and her insurance will skyrocket. All of this assumes that she returns."

Phase One accomplished. Except for Tommy's major mishap, all is well. The consequences of Tommy's rash reaction won't cause us to alter our plans. I must be ironclad in my resolve and very alert to his actions during the next few days. I'm not sure what has to be done with him.

ANY WEDNESDAY

The hotel at the Denver airport is ideal for my purpose. Collapse and arise before dawn. Be on the road early. Have to arrive at the Albuquerque airport by 4 so I can be met by Ahmed and become a new person. Drive will take 7-8 hours. Simple Rental deals in one-way rentals from airport to airport anywhere in the west. They rent neat cars. Not the family fare of the majors. Ellie shuffles to the car, tosses her body in the passenger seat of the Dodge Viper. Her face weirdly resembles that of a winning fighter . . . red and puffy. Black and blue will come soon. She curls up and tries to sleep.

"We'll stop for breakfast once we're clear of Denver."

"Yeah, whatever."

On the road before seven. Cruise control set for 70. Now the tough part. Find an acceptable radio station. No western cowboy. No songs of faith. No proselytizing screamers. No talk or all-sports. I want an oldies' station. *KBTT . . . Kick butt radio. The music you grew up with.* The DJ is very hyper, but he plays four in a row before the onslaught of very bad local advertising. I never ran radio ads for the *Bric's Hardware Store.* Once a quarter we ran any advertising in the newspaper with money from the manufacturers passed through the wholesalers. It's where Gustafson and I generated personal cash flow. The sun is getting hot on the windshield. 9:45. Time to break for breakfast. Denny's at next exit.

"Ellie. Ellie. Ellie. It's time to wake up. Open your eyes and take a big stretch. We're gonna' stop for breakfast. Wake up."

"Whew. That was a deep sleep. Strange dream. We were out on the boat at home. Big storm blew up real quick, like the ones in the fall. Black clouds and lots of wind. Boat was like a toy in a tub. We scrambled to put on our life vests. Waves came over the side, but we didn't take on much water. The lake was as cold as ever, but the air was warm . . . almost hot.

You wanted me to tie onto the rail and sit. I wanted to work. There was a lot I had to below deck. We argued. Water crashed over us, and I was pitched overboard. You called out my name, but I couldn't see you because of the waves and the darkness. Funny, you weren't yelling, you were just speaking softly to me, but I could still hear you over the storm's noise. Then I awoke. Weird."

The parking lot is filled with the expected big rigs, campers, SUV's and pick-up trucks. The Chrysler Prowler is an obvious tourist give away.

"What can I get you, two, today . . ."

Coffee is waiting beside the enormously complex menus. Ellie departs upon my arrival.

Hit with the hypnotist's cue-like phrase, I zone out and am oblivious to my surroundings. Only to be awakened when I am behind the wheel. Ellie settles in for more sleep. I think she is taking more than pain pills.

* *

Get to the airport. Call the motel. Ahmed arrives. Exchange banalities. Swap cash for two sets of ID's and one gun. I have become Bob Welch. My wife is Elaine. Pay him for the other ID's and two more guns. I'll meet the other planes. Ahmed's traveling companion is a young woman he calls Cheeka. She nods at the introduction. Does not smile and never takes her eyes away from Ahmed except to scan the area around him. She is human radar seeking out possible harm.

Despite the temperature, she wears a mid thigh lightweight leather jacket. It is sufficiently loose fitting to conceal the contours of her upper body and any weapon or weapons she might carry. Her neck is solid like a lifter's and her hands are not delicate despite the polish and obvious professional attention. Ahmed needs to make the connection. He and Cheeka will be back. Swim, nap, and wait. Marilee is the first of the crew to arrive. She becomes Maggie, wife of Tim Conrad.

She looks almost invigorated by the event. The new Jaqa and Tariq Richard arrive about ten PM. They are good to go. Tim will arrive tomorrow at 7 AM. Tariq and Ahmed spend time catching up on their families. Jaqa is not with them, but Cheeka is. Everybody is properly outfitted. All of their old identities are handed over and destroyed. We must burn our new names into our brains so that they become natural in our conversations. We can never slip up.

"Ahmed made the connection. He is waiting to call back about time and place. Eighteen for three hundred and fifty is no problem. All we can do is wait."

"Tariq, I don't want to sit around the motel more than another day. Otherwise, someone will get suspicious. Did you remind Ahmed of my timetable?"

"Yes, and he expects to speak to the Mexicans before noon. He said the Mexicans are just as interested as we are to do the deal and split. They need to keep a lower profile that we do. But, they need to check his credentials so that they can accept whom he recommends. This entire business is done on the basis of who knows whom and who can you trust. Once the Mexicans are convinced that they can trust Ahmed, they will trust us. Still, Ahmed told me there will probably be about a half dozen Mexicans and they will be armed. Trust only goes so far."

"Before he talks to the Mexicans, we need to tell Ahmed we want two things. We want to check purity. I want 90% pure and nothing less. Anything less jeopardizes our ability to step on the smack and get more for the money. Second, we want to do the deal in a public place. Ideally with other people around."

"Sampling will delay the final transaction."

"So be it. I don't want to get stiffed by a bunch of beaners, because they thought we were too dumb to ask."

"OK, you're the boss. But, how are we going to test the purity?"

"I'll bet Ahmed has the testing chemicals. He brought enough cutting powder and packets for the second phase of our venture. That cost us ten grand, but we don't have to worry about people getting suspicious of strange purchases. I think he's going to buy for himself or for his crew in LA. In fact, I would not be very surprised if he is buying off our cash. I mean, who says the price is 20 a kee. Ahmed says. Maybe it's really 18 a kee. If it's we pay 20, Ahmed kicks in 40 and he buys a total of twenty-two with our money. We get eighteen and he keeps four. He buys off our money and we're never the wiser."

"He wouldn't cheat family."

"Stop and think for a moment how stupid that sounds. Think of Ahmed as a drug dealer. Think of Ahmed as a distant relative with a truly counter lifestyle. A distant relative, with whom you haven't had face-to-face contact in years. He is a fucking stranger, who would cheat you and me to make the kind of money that's going to be on the table. I am willing to look the other way and let him run his game so long as we get twelve kees of 90% purity. That way we can sell a ton of shit in Minneapolis.

At 50 per, our goal is easily attainable. Also, we need to do the deal where rooftop shooters can't surprise us. And a farm field is not an acceptable venue. I don't want a bunch of Zapata's jumping out from behind cactus, shooting us, and leaving with our cash and their drugs. If they know that we know what could happen, they will be more likely to deal with us as almost peers. Now, make sure Ahmed is clear as to what I want. Your ability to convey that to him is critical to the success of this phase."

"Consider it done. Question. Have you and Elaine talked about what she might be planning to do after we sell in Minneapolis?"

"No, and right now I don't want to be distracted by an array of possibilities. All of us must remain focused on the tasks at hand. Otherwise the operation will fail. We've already had one serious screw up. It altered our course somewhat. We cannot afford another. Mental distraction will cause an error."

"I don't know what to think about Jaqa and our future."

"My suggestion is to not think about it. You two either have a future or you don't and there is not much you can do about it. Your future with your wife depends on what she wants to do. So leave it alone for now. Plan to have a long talk with her after Minneapolis."

"I guess you're right. I'll go tell Ahmed what we discussed."

The length of the day was taking its toll. I plopped onto the bed and put my feet up. Elaine was in Maggie's room. The television was warming the corner of ours. Suddenly I am awakened by a noise at the door.

* *

"Bob, honey let me in. I left my keys on the bathroom counter."

"Hey there. I was just dozing off. How's Maggie?"

"She seems to be OK. In fact, she seems to be better than OK. It's like ever since she decided this thing was a good idea, she's come out of her shell. You know all the times the four of us were together; she never opened up about anything really personal. The things woman love to hear and discuss in the strictest of confidence never on her lips. It was like she endured the dull existence of school administrator only to come home to the dull life with her mate. But, now she is in a tell-all mood. I mean, I have learned things about Tim that I would have never thought of."

"Elaine, I don't care about their lives. I only care that they perform their tasks. And, right now Tim is on my watch closely list. He fucked up once. We can't afford another. So, while I'm happy that Maggie is coming out of her chrysalis, I want to be sure she doesn't mess up. I want you to sit with her and go over exactly what she will be responsible for after we buy the stuff. She will be driving the smack back to Minneapolis. She will be the mule hidden in plain sight.

In a car for two 12-hour days is difficult. Although she'll have Tim as a passenger, she will be responsible for delivery. Tomorrow I'll get two walkie-talkies for the trip so we can talk if need be. They'll be the kind hikers take on long trips.

A range of up to 15 miles. So if one of us has a flat tire or an emergency stop, or, God forbid, sees a police roadblock we can talk. But, I don't want an open-ended cross-country dialogue. I have the map for her trip. The places where we will meet based on gas mileage. I want you to make sure she understands that we are counting on her. Not Tim. Her."

"I can do that."

"Great. I'm exhausted. I'd like to turn in. You can stay up if you want."

"I think I'd like to snuggle."

Elaine's euphemism for foreplay. Hell, I don't mind. The change in our emotional relationship is permanent. But, we can be physical. Physical is always good. Whatever gets me through the night.

* *

Back at the airports to pick up Tim. He looks ready for some kind of cowboy wannabe in an action flick. He is wearing genuine cowboy dress-up duds. Denim pants with silver studs, and a red and black pearl-buttoned shirt. Black boots with turquoise and silver inlay and a huge gold and silver buckled belt. The black hat that nearly covers his ears and eyes makes him look like a caricature. One of those drawings at fairs and carnivals. Distorted face and a strange costume. The outfit looks very expensive. If all the stuff is real, it probably set him back two grand. Is that how he spent is traveling money?

"Hey man, are we ready to rock and roll?"

"Just a few details to iron out."

"What do you think of the threads? Neat, eh?"

"They certainly make a statement."

He was begging for money a few days ago. Now it looks like he spent two month's pay on his clothes.

"My bag will be at Carousel C. Then we can get goin'. I'm lookin' forward to doin' the deal and makin' the sale. By the way, who am I now?"

"Tim Conrad. You'll need to sign the cards and we'll get them laminated. Plus, give me your old wallet and all the personal stuff in it. Everything must be destroyed. We can dump your old persona into the flames of the trash heap behind the motel. I paid the balance for your ID's. You can bounce me back after the Twin Cities. I'll keep a tab."

"When do we make the buy?"

"Ahmed will have an answer by noon. My hope is to make the buy this evening and leave for the long drive tomorrow morning. But, it's out of my control."

His bag looked more expensive than his clothes. He flashed the money. Just like I told him not to. The cab ride back to the motel was quiet. He is definitely a risk to be watched. Not sure about Maggie. Maybe I've entrusted too much to these two. If I don't tell him what he has in the trunk of the car, I can probably reduce the risk of him screwing up. How tough can it be to simply drive from one place to another?

* *

"Good news. We can make the connection this afternoon. The Mexicans want to get home. I think they feel heat. We'll meet at 4 at the fountain in the center of the Tierra Verde Mall. They'll have a sample for us there."

"Ahmed, it sounds like a set-up. They are playing us for amateurs. How would we be able to test anything out in the open? I bet we'll meet there and they'll tell us they stuff is somewhere else. Just a short drive away. We're at risk when we go with them, because we'll be going into their den. Daniel had to go into the lion's den. I don't have to. So we'll play the same game.

Take a taste of the cash and tell them the rest is elsewhere. We can test their shit in your car. They can have the cash. There has got to be a construction site near the mall. Some housing development, where the workers quit by four. We can have all the cash there . . . in a car with the ladies. They can meet us and we'll complete the deal. Cars. Shit, I almost forgot. We got yours, Ahmed. But, we'll need two more. Once the deal is done, we're splitting."

"I noticed in the newspaper this morning a couple of Buy-Here-Pay-Here car lots. I bet we can go there and pay cash and drive off the lot. Jaqa and I can handle that. Bob, do you have any cash for this deal? I have about ten. May need more. We'll be back here by 2. OK? Ahmed, can you drive us to the first lot?"

"Tariq, here's six. Buy a van and a sedan."

"Cheeka and I can take you."

"Great. Don't ask or tell Tim what we're doing. And, make sure you guys pack and leave everything in our room. I'll checkout the crew. See you by 2. I want to scout the area around the mall for a housing development before we meet our new business partners."

Some times I feel like a combination Army Captain and schoolteacher. I have to tell them what to do and when to do it. Only Tariq takes any initiative. I better rely on him more as this activity progresses. I can delegate to him. He can ride herd on Tim and Maggie. He can take the stress from my shoulders. Four are off on missions. Elaine explaining Maggie's duties. Tim and I set off to buy walkie-talkies. Ostensibly for our climb in the mountains. The Gear Shop has what we need. Tim also buys a large knife . . . an ornate, gem encrusted handle and twelve-inch blade, razor sharp on one side and serrated on the other. Three hundred dollars for a large piece of jewelry. The final details of his proclivity to fuck up are painting a dangerous picture.

* *

At 1:30 Tariq and Jaqa arrive with our transportation . . . a six-year old Chevy Camaro and a four-year old Dodge Caravan. Tariq spent less than fourteen. Cash works wonders. We exit the motel and load our luggage. The moneybag sits in the trunk of the Camaro to be driven by Maggie. Off to the mall.

The Estates of Grande Sierra . . . Homes from the low $200's. Reduced to sell.

Perfect. Only two crews working. They'll all be gone by 4. Maggie will look like another prospect. We will meet her at 3434 Rio Vista, a sprawling jumble of pipes, planks, dry wall and exterior stucco far away from the development's entrance. Grab a bite to eat and head to the mall. Tim keeps touching his gun, like a small child touching his penis to make sure it is still there.

It's 3:30. Elaine remains in the Caravan and Jaqa stays in Ahmed's Infinity, while Ahmed and his troops go to the fountain. Cheeka, Tim, and Tariq mingle in the sparse weekday crowd around the fountain and in the shops

"Guys, just a word. Mexican druggies operate on their own time. Don't be surprised if they keep us waiting at least an hour."

"Should I tell our drivers so they don't get nervous?"

"Yeah."

* *

We wait. And wait. The fountain is the center of the mall. The base is about sixty feet in diameter. Water spouts twenty feet and splashes down indigenous rocks to the pond and to be recycled. About twenty four-seater benches are scattered around the base in a randomly planned mode. The dome is another twenty feet above the spew of water. And the area is loaded with lush, non-native flora. A jungle motif in the desert. Plus, the birds. Multi-colored cacophony.

All-in-all true sensory discordance . . . frenetic human motion and bird noises counter the lush moistness of the garden. The general population of the mall is split between those under eighteen and those over fifty-five. Many more women than men. All seem to be dressed for walking and being seen. Sneakers and cut-off jeans and very skimpy tops for the teens and sneakers, loose fitting sundresses, jewelry, and too much make up for the AARP set. We wait. I notice groups of girls make the fountain sort of a base. They meet here and then head down one of the three radii, only to return, regroup and head down another radius. Rats on a treadmill make better progress. But they look happy, so who am I to criticize.

Ahmed rises and strolls toward two short dark-skinned men dressed in dark green from shoes to collar. They look like they are products of the surrounding plants. Some form of mutant strain. A *pluman* or *huant*. The conversation of the three is calm until one of the *plumans* shakes his little head three times. The answer is no. Then he talks to Ahmed, who responds in kind. Finally, there is agreement and hand shaking all around. The *huants,* joined by four other *plumans*, who seeped from the underbrush near the shops, amble down the East radius.

"They will meet us at the construction site in one hour. Call Maggie and tell her to move to a location away from the site. I'm sure the Mexicans will place men strategically around the place. We want her to be outside their ring of security. Meanwhile, we'll test the shit."

"The redder the blue . . . the richer the color of the liquid, the purer the shit. Yahoo. Look. The color of the Pope's Easter robe. About 90% pure I would guess. Worth the price. Hell, you could step on this shit more than once and still sell smack the junkies on the street would consider primo. Shall we close the deal?"

* *

We arrive at the appointed construction site and wait again.

"Don't turn now, but in a minute look to your right at the second story of the house in the next lot. The back window. If you're lucky, you'll see a small person who probably has a big rifle. So they are set. When they feel we have no one to act as security, and that we are all within their ring, they will come to the table. Do not show your weapons. When they arrive make sure you stand next to one of the men. Consider your partner a possible shield and immediate target if things get dicey.

Do not make any sudden moves. Let me do all the moving. Sudden motions spook these guys and their reaction is to shoot everybody . . . sometimes their own. But, if it is necessary to draw our weapons, the impact of intent is clearer when you're closer. So find a dance partner right away."

We wait. Two women in cars outside and four men and a woman inside the shell of a house. Our cash is nowhere near. We all wait. Two black BMW sedans pull up to the site. Windows are blacked out. Doors open and out ooze eight *plumans*. I wonder if the K-Mart in Guadalajara was running a sale on ugly dark green clothes. *Dress your entire family of eight for only 3,000 pesos.* Two stand by the car and six enter the house-to-be. One guy has two, anodized attaché cases. These are set on the carpenter's Band saw table.

"Thank you for coming. Allow my associate to summon the money."

I wave to Elaine to call Maggie. The Camaro arrives in three minutes. Maggie, carrying one of the L.L. Bean bags, enters the sticks and stucco site. She places the bag on the saw table and leaves quickly. The three containers sit on the altar of transaction. I approach the metal cases as one of the *huants* opens the moneybag.

It's always polite to let the guest go first. He counts. I count. I get eleven in each case. Twenty-two total. I was right. Ahmed was buying with our money. Before he is done counting, Ahmed hands a soft leather bag to the head *pluman*. He looks inside, appears satisfied, and closes the bag. The counter is done and zips the bag. Eyes dart around the space. The sun is on its way to the Orient. As the bagman turns and heads for the car, the other five cautiously back up. Tim seems to leap at me. His face beaming and his arms waving.

"Hey, man we did it. We got the goods. Now, let's get out of Dodge."

The first shot comes from the house next door. It strikes Cheeka in the lower back. She bounces to the concrete slab, pulls her Tech-9 and begins to spray at the *plumans*. The second rifle shot comes from the back of the site and smashes into a two-by-four next to Tariq. He has already drawn his gun and is firing as he moves for some form of cover. The Mexicans are beating a hasty retreat and firing back at the house. By the time I realize we are in the epicenter of a firefight I am kneeling behind a stack of wallboard.

Ahmed is leaning on a sawhorse, trying to right himself. Each time he arises someone hits him from somewhere. Cheeka is slithering over to her boss and re-loading her Tech-9. She gets off another spray in the direction of the fleeing dealers, but slumps to the concrete slab as one of their shots luckily finds her. Tariq scoots to his cousin and tries to pull him off the horse and behind a stack of stucco bags. As Tariq lifts Ahmed's body, he spins like a top. The first shot comes from the guys running away, the second from the back yard, and the third from one of the *huants* who has been hiding at the front door.

I guess he is to be the rear guard. As he stands in the doorway to complete Tariq's execution, I get off six rounds. At least four find the silhouette. It appears to be yanked out of the door way and into the front yard. The two black BMWs roar off into the evening. After the explosion of noise and confusion, the silence is frightening. No groaning. In the dying sunlight, dark pools are visible beneath and around the bodies.

"Tariq? Tim? Cheeka? Ahmed? Is anybody still here?"

"Bob, are you OK?"

"Tim, check Cheeka to see if she is alive. I'll check Tariq and Ahmed."

"She is dead. No pulse."

I look into two faces. Cousins, who lived in different worlds. Killed by one of the worlds. Four eyes rolled back. No pulses. Two dead. I remove Tariq's gun.

"Holy shit, Bric, check out the bodies. We got three."

"Four. There's one outside. Tim, give me your gun and go to the cars. Tell the ladies that its time to leave. Take the drugs and put the two cases in the Chevy. Maggie has a walkie-talkie. Elaine has one in the Caravan. Jaqa, Elaine and I will catch up to you and Maggie at rest stop three. Tell Maggie rest stop number three. Also, tell Jaqa to come in here if she wants to pay her last respects to Tariq. Tell Elaine I'll be along shortly. You and Maggie head to the Interstate. Now!"

I take his piece with two fingers pinched at the edge of the clip. It is cold. It's not been fired. I note that Tim has a large wet spot in the crotch of his jeans. The fucking coward just hid and peed himself. He was of no use in the fight. Worse, his action started the fight and his non-action probably got someone killed. If he had fired, he could have hit someone. Or distracted somebody. Maybe he could have saved Tariq. Damn and Tariq was worth saving.

That's two fuck-ups. And, two are two too many. I am careful not to disturb anything on his gun. I wrap it in a piece of cloth found by the saw. I now have all three guns. I may need them later. Seven dead and a fancy car outside. The police will have a picnic. They'll figure out this was a drug deal gone bad, run prints and mug shots, and know exactly who was left behind. Then trace Tariq back to Duluth and us. Our window of opportunity will slam shut on our necks. The second safety hatch is locked.

"Bob, are you sure he's dead?"

"Yes, all three are dead."

"He tried to be good for me, but I wasn't good for him. Maybe it's better this way. We won't have to fight about his disappointment. Two questions. Will I get his share? What will happen to the bodies?"

"His share will be dumped back into the pot and distributed equally among those who remain. And I'll take care of the bodies. You should leave now. Tell Elaine I'll meet you guys at rest stop number noted on the Interstate. We will leave my car there, and then the three of us will meet Tim and Maggie at rest stop number three. Is that clear? I'll meet you two at two. I should be there about a half-hour after you guys get there. Just stay in the car and wait for me. OK? Now go. We have a lot to do before this is finally over."

I hear the van leave. I search for the circuit breaker box and turn on the juice. Then I lift Cheeka onto the band saw table. She is a wobbly, floppy load. As cold in death as she appeared in life. I turn on the saw and slide her into position. Before eliminating the traceable evidence, I grab the plastic wrap that encased the stucco bags when they were on the skid. This goes between the saw table and me from my feet to my shoulders. A very large pancho. Slowly I push Cheeka's right wrist through the band of jagged steel. The shredding of her wrist sprinkles blood and bits of flesh and bone all over the workspace. Then I do the left wrist. Then her neck. The crunching of the large bones sounds like the sizing of a wood plank. The splattering of blood and small parts cover my makeshift pancho. The second traceable personality to disappear is Tariq. The blood and bits layer the plastic.

Ahmed slides through the saw with ease because I know where to cut. I fold up my cover. The police will now find a horrible mess. Four Mexicans and three headless, handless blacks. There will be no way to trace the victims of this horrific episode. Turn off the saw and flick the breaker. Wipe it clean. Wipe the saw handle and switch. Put the six hands and three heads into the plastic sheet. Search the bodies for wallets and other traceable items. Retrieve Ahmed's car keys. Wash my face, hair, and hands at the outdoor hose. Strip, except for my boxers, T-shirt, and socks. Toss my clothes in with the body parts. Put three guns on the passenger seat. The bloody bag goes thud in the trunk of Ahmed's Infinity, and I head for rest stop two on the Interstate.

THURSDAY WORK NIGHT

"Follow me."

The two cars snake to the rear of the long-term parking at our designated rest stop number two. In the middle of a row of campers and RV's left by hikers, I deposit Ahmed's Infinity. I like this car so much; I may have to get one when this is all over. Elaine pulls behind my meat wagon.

I lower the driver's side window.

"Go to my bag and get me a pair of shoes, socks, khakis, and a pullover, please."

"Well don't we look special? Do you get some kind of kick driving in your tightie whities? I'll bet you cruise these parking lots looking for lonely women."

"Cut the crap and get me my clothes."

Despite the awkwardness of dressing while seated at the business point of a car, I'm outside and lacing my sneakers in less than two minutes. Two guns tucked in the back of my belt. One wrapped in cloth in my pocket. Wipe the car of my prints. Lock the car and toss the keys down a ravine beyond the guardrail. The stench of rotting body parts will not be obvious for two days. We will be safe at home by then. Jaqa slides open a side door of the van and I jump in. put all three guns in my bag.

"OK, troops. Next stop rest stop number three. That's 125 miles, less than two hours from here. We'll meet up with Tim and Maggie there."

"What did you do with the bodies?"

"Suffice it to say that the police will find more corpses than traceable bodies. The scene will look like two rivals had a big shoot 'em up over drugs. It will look as if the Mexicans lost a few soldiers when the deal went south. So, they took out their rage on the Blacks. Try not to worry or think about it. We are all free and clear of the phase. Now, I'd like to get some sleep. I'll drive after we meet up with Maggie and Tim."

* *

The exhaustion of the day and the rhythmic bump-click of the tires over the concrete slabs of the road make a devastating combination. I am groggy in ten minutes and fast asleep soon thereafter.

Jerking of the vehicle and cries of "hello" wake me. The cramp in my body tells me I slept on the bench seat. The drool puddle on the seat told me I slept soundly. The four of them are in back of the Caravan.

"Elaine. Jaqa. Are you guys OK?"

"Everybody who is here is fine."

"Tim told me of the terrible gun fight. Sort of like the OK Corral. Where's Bob?"

"Here I am."

Maggie bounces up to me and gives me an unexpected full-body hug with a touch of hip grind for good measure.

"I'm so glad you're safe. Tim told me about how you two had to fight your way out of the mess the Mexicans made. Bob, what's next?"

"The Twin Cities is our goal. And here's how we get there. We drive for another four hours. There is a major exit with numerous motels about two hundred and eighty miles from here. When we exit, Tim and Maggie will go to one motel . . . any motel. We will go to another . . . any other. We can't look like we're together. So we can't drive as convoy. But, not too far apart. No more than ten miles or ten minutes. That's the range of the walkie-talkies. You two leave this rest stop and we'll follow. I need something to eat. Before we exit up the road, we can talk on the boxes. Is all that clear?"

Rest stop food is as predictable as the road we're on. I drive the next leg.

"Jaqa. Elaine. The sixty-four dollar question for us deals with room assignments. If you two would like to share a room, that's OK with me. Elaine, if you want to share accommodations with me that's OK, also. It's your choice. Your decision. Now is the time to make an open commitment."

The sense of discomfort emanates from the pair like sweat on the forehead of a condemned man. Elaine turns to the back seat. I can see in the rearview mirror, the pleading in Jaqa's eyes. A small child, who needs to be held after a big scare or bad accident, Elaine puts her hand on mine to seek approval. I squeeze back to her.

"I'll stay with Jaqa tonight."

The door to any future relationship is locked.

"Since we got an early start on the long trip home, we will have plenty time to cut and bag the heroin. I think we should do some of it tomorrow night and the balance when we are in Minneapolis. That way there is no deadline panic. Jaqa, call Maggie and tell her to take the attaché cases into her room and then call me."

"Are we supposed to say 10-4 on these damn things? Do we need code names?"

"They're called handles, and 10-4 is not necessary. What would you like as a handle?"

"I'll be Black Bird. Maggie can be Snow Bird."

"Tell her that."

"Snow Bird, this is Black Bird. Do you hear me?"

"Black Bird, this is Snow Bird. Neat. Just like in the army. I hear you."

"Snow Bird, where do you plan to nest?"

"We will check into Motel 6 about two miles north of exit 34. There are a bunch of motels south of the exit. I have all this on the map."

"Big Bird wants you to call him when you're flight is over."

"OK. Over and out."

The conversation is reminiscent of those children have with two cans and a taut piece of string. But, the message is heard and acknowledged. The rest of the drive is sort of point and shoot.

* *

"Bob, sweetie, exit 34 is 38 miles ahead."

Elaine's use of the affectionate is a disturbing hangover from our years together. I'm sure she is unaware she even said it.

Two rooms. I am the loner. I agree to meet Maggie at her motel.

* *

"What's happnin'?"

"I'm worried about Tim. He drank a bottle of bourbon during the drive. And all he spoke about was how much you must hate him. I couldn't get the details from him, but he scared me with his ranting. I know that all our actions are important to the success of what we are doing. Everybody's equally important. I am afraid Tim is coming unglued, and that he could do something stupid to fuck up our operation. I don't want that. This is my chance to get out and start fresh. What was Tim so upset about?"

"He didn't perform his duties at the sale with the Mexicans. In fact he fucked up. He instigated the gunfight. Then he never fired his gun in defense of Cheeka, Tariq, or Ahmed. The net of his actions and absence of them is that people got killed. And, this was not the first time. He killed a guard in the bank truck. I'm not entirely convinced that shooting was necessary. Regardless, Tim went beyond the prescribed course of action. We were to spray and hit . . . not shoot. He is closing and locking our escape hatches at every step. I have the sinking feeling Tim can't be trusted and that his future actions will expose us to an even greater risk of discovery. But, I'm not sure what to do about it yet."

"Let me be honest with you, Bob. During the past two years, and particularly the last six months, Tim has drifted away from me. Emotionally and physically. I know he didn't love his work, but the pay and benefits were decent. So, he should have sucked it upped and looked for something better. Like this. Until then he could have made the best of his situation. His ego began to emerge as a twisted force. When he drank, and that was often, the conversation seemed to center on high school athletics. How he was the captain of the football and basketball teams. How he led both teams to the regional finals. How scouts were hinting at scholarships ... Big Ten, Big Twelve.

The reality of his grades and three-digit SAT score put an end to his dream. It was someone else's fault he didn't go to college. His teachers were no good. He never got a chance for extra help. Every once and a while he would remind me how lucky I was to catch him. How he could have been with any other girl. Hell, he even told me their names. And the places. He started to gamble heavily up at the reservation. He'd go up to the Casino and lose. I'm not sure how much he lost. We never spoke about that. I think he was stealing from the company for gambling money. At first he claimed he was being paid for the overtime and the weekends.

About three months ago he confessed, the company didn't pay him for the OT, but was going to give him a big bonus at the end of the year. Then everything would be all right. Also, I figured out that each time he went into the plant on Saturday; the same two bimbos were there. Our sex life drifted to nothing. So with the booze, the wasted money, the ton of self-pity, and the off-campus interludes, he was pulling a shell over his head. I don't think we've had a conversation about anything important since the fall. Then this."

"Did this change him?"

"He claimed that he was focussing on his part, but he was lost. I even had to remind him of the simple tasks you gave him. So he drifted farther away from me. And the irony is that I am becoming alive. I am excited about this plan. The plan has unleashed feelings I never dreamed I had. Look at me. I have changed. My clothes. My hair and make up. My whole attitude has changed to be focussed on me. I need this plan to succeed. And ..."

"And ..."

"I don't need Tim to screw up my future like he screwed up my life so far. I deserve something better than the loser he has become. I deserve to be with a winner. What do you have to say about all that?"

"I'm sorry Tim has not lived up to your expectations. I'm keeping my eyes on him to make sure he does what I expect from here on out. I haven't decided what to do about the two incidents. Maybe I should just forget they happened and move on."

"What about me?"

"I will rely on you to be the strong one of the couple. I will rely on you to report his actions and conversations to me. Tariq was strong. He was my lieutenant. Now he's dead, you can have that responsibility."

"No, you missed the point. What about me as a woman? I know what is going on between Jaqa and Elaine. You know what is not going on between Tim and me. Nothing. Why can't there be something going on between you and me? I need it and you deserve it."

"I, we, can't afford to lose focus. Tim has lost focus. The lovers appear to be looking to their future with only an occasional glimpse at today. If we were to become involved now, our emotions would interfere with our minds. We might not think clearly. So, regardless of what you may want, we have to work together not sleep together."

"Another man brushes me off. Jesus, I'm getting a complex. Am I such a toad that no guy wants to be with me?"

"No. You're desirable. But, I will not let my little head rule my big one. I must wait until the end of this project before I become rightfully self-indulgent. I'll have the luxury of time and money to decide what I want to do. You will have this same luxury. Can you wait? Hell it's only a few more days."

"Yes, I can wait. Fuck! I hate it when someone else is right. And you are right. Oh well, on to business. We have two cases each with the bags in them. A total of 22 kilograms of Black Tar Heroin. And, we have all the necessary material to cut only four of the bags the heroin into 8,000 one-gram packets. That Herculean task will take most night if not all of it and then some. What should we do with the kilos we can't cut and repackage?"

"Tomorrow night, we'll start the process. We'll take four kees and mix it with the cutting powder. We'll make as many street packets as we can that night and re-bag the balance. So will have some uncut. Some cut in big bags. And some cut in street-ready packets. We'll ask for 2 million dollars for the total. Hell, that's a real bargain. Some shit can be moved the day after the buy. Some can be moved the next week and some next month. Or resold to another distributor. Elaine will have to alert her contact as to the final quantity."

"It's going to take a lot of time to break down that much, but we can do it. It's settled then; the job comes before I do. Before you head back to your empty bed, I want you to see what you're missing."

She leans into my face and kisses me deeply.

"Good night, my Captain."

I sleep secure in the knowledge that I have an able lieutenant and that my plan for Tim is the right one. Just when and where?

* *

Breakfast is silent. We decide to split the driving every four hours. Elaine takes the first shift. My concern centers on Maggie. Will she be able to make such a long trip being the sole driver? If she can make it, will she be able to work the night shift of cutting and bagging? Should Elaine or Jaqa spell her at the wheel of the Camaro? Me? When Jaqa takes over, Elaine will drive for Maggie. It's the only way to lessen Maggie's load. The scenery is magnificent. But, all we can do is look as we drive by. Can't touch. Another time I should come back and take excursions. During Elaine's shift the time neither moves nor stands still. It is. We break for coffee, a stretch, and a new driver . . . me.

"Jaqa, call Maggie, and ask her how she's doin'. Tell her Elaine will spell her at the next break. We should plan to meet somewhere in Missouri."

"Snow Bird. This is Black Bird. Do you copy?"

"Black Bird. This is Snow Bird. I copy."

"How's it going'?"

"Tediously."

"Big Bird decided that you deserve a break today. Lady Bird will take over your responsibilities. We will meet somewhere in Missouri. Do you copy?"

"Yes, and thank Big Bird and Lady Bird for me. Eight hours is about all I can do at one stretch. Where specifically should we meet?"

"According to the map, rest stop number 4-A about a hundred miles below the Iowa line seems to be ideal. We'll meet, Elaine will get into your car, and we'll decide our next step. Got that?"

"Rest stop 4-A. See you there between three and four this afternoon. Over and out."

* *

It seems as if we have been in flatland for about a year. Interstate numbers run together . . . 25, 40, 44, 70, 35, and all the three-digit variations that circle cities. The farms all look alike. The houses the barns were all crafted from the same plans. The motels never change. The constant parade of SUV's and RV's. The biggest difference between the states is the police cars. Colors, markings, and exterior accoutrements . . . lights and antennae. Otherwise the trip is visually monotonous.

We decide to play the license plate game. The object is to note the license plates of different states. The person who has the most confirmed "kills" wins. The prize is fifty bucks each from the other two. To further sweeten the game, five dollars from each will be awarded to anyone, who spots an Alaskan plate and ten for a Hawaiian plate. Jaqa divvies up the pencils and sheets of paper. Cars from the Southwest, Deep South, and Plains states are easy. East Coast, New England, and West Coast are sparse. But, it occupies time. We agree that Maggie and Tim should be not involved. We're kids again riding in the back seats of over-stuffed Buick's, and Mercury's screaming with glee at every new plate. Despite the explosions, our parents must have been pleased that we were occupied and not pestering them.

"Rest stop 4-A is the next one. Jaqa, call Maggie see where she is now."

The call-and-identification sequence is repeated. Maggie is about to pull into the rest stop. Three times she claims to be fine. Obviously she is not. Am I the only one who hears her distress?

The stop is not crowded. It's too early for dinner and too late for lunch. Park and stretch. Tim remains in the car.

"Hey, I really appreciate the break form the wheel. Shall we eat before we head out?"

"Before we do all that, let's figure where we will stop for the night. We have a lot of work, so maybe we should drive only two hours. Any suggestions?"

"Let's go until six. We can work for eight hours, sleep, and get back on the road early. Then we can finish our work in Minneapolis tomorrow night, and make the delivery the day after. Then we can all disappear."

Maggie is asserting herself. Elaine and Jaqa just nod. Like children, they run giggling toward the *Brunchland* eatery.

"Tim is a lost cause. He just sleeps in the back section. Every so often he mumbles something about how it's not his fault. How he is better than I think or you think. How he has to do something to show us just how good he is. Frankly, I don't trust him. He may snap and do something really stupid. That one act that would queer the entire deal. I don't know what it is, but I do know he is capable of doing it. What are we going to do?"

Maggie speaks in slow muted urgency. Her eyes manifest concern ... deep concern.

"I'll have to take care of the problem at the appropriate time. You understand what that will entail?"

"Yes. I think so."

"Do you think he wants anything to eat or drink?"

"I'll wake him and get him inside."

"Do you think he'll be able to help us tonight and in Minneapolis?"

"No."

"Then we, you and I, have to keep a watchful eye on him for the next thirty-six hours. He must never be out of our sight, except when he sleeps. And then we should check on him every few hours. We must limit our risk for the big reward. Let's join the others for something to eat?"

"I'm so damned anxious about him that I'm not sure I'm hungry."

"You must eat. This plan needs you to be strong."

Our meal contains more cholesterol than I would eat in a month. Three eggs, bacon, sausage, home fries, and biscuits with gravy. Thank God I'm not driving. My body will collapse into a nap. I call the TC Motor Lodge and reserve three rooms for tomorrow. Elaine calls her friend to set up the connection. Tim wanders to the newsstand, purchases *USA Today* and heads to the bathroom. His toilet regimen delays us twenty minutes. We wait in the cars.

* *

"Sharon says she can do the deal, but needs an extra day to get that much money together. We speak in such weird code. I think that's what she was saying. But, I'm to call her again tomorrow between noon and one at the hospital. She claims the hospital is safe. All looks good."

Is Sharon setting a trap? Our next stop, Budgetel . . . 148 miles.

* *

Three rooms. Mine is the single. Agreed: shower and meet in my room in forty minutes. Tim will not be joining us. He needs his sleep. I have the bags and bagging material and equipment.

The air system is turned off. Air currents are a danger to spew the merchandise. Towels are wrapped over the table and taped underneath. Wax paper is spread across the towels and taped so there are no gaps. The surface allows us to scoop, without cutting the paper. Four stainless steel whisks, and four small aluminum-measuring spoons are washed and dried with toilet paper. Everyone wears disposable surgical gloves and masks, as well as plastic bibs. Nothing is to stick to anything or be inhaled by us.

All four kees of the heroin are poured into the center of the table and spread around in a layer. I sprinkle the cutting powder over the bed of smack. The four of us slowly whisk and fold the powdered mixture, blending it like a flan. The first phase is deliberately slow. It takes an hour. Break time. Each of us has accumulated sweat behind the bib and on the forehead. No air. Hot light. Concentration. The process is executed with precision for three hours.

"I gotta' pee."

Elaine's bladder has never been strong. And it gets weaker with excitement.

"What about Tim?"

"He's sleeping off his load. We'll see him in the morning."

"Jaqa, do you want coffee?"

"Thanks. Guys, we should wear bandanas to keep the sweat away from our eyes. I'll make them out of hand towels."

Break over, we return to our stations. Each fills a measuring spoon to level by shaking off the excess, inserts the spoon into the maw of the small bag, tips the spoon, taps the spoon through the plastic with our middle finger, extracts the spoon, seals the bag, and places a market-ready product into a large ziplock bag sitting in our laps. We are the assembly line. The first hundred procedures are slow and awkward. We are careful not to make a mistake.

The desire to complete this phase, the ease of our newfound task, and the repetition allow us to accelerate the tempo of work, ever cautious that only the measuring spoon may touch the powder. Once a comfortable rate is established we settle into the routine of the task at hand. In this new phase, time rushes by. Another three hours.

"Break time. Coffee or pop?"

"Elaine, want some coffee?"

"I'll count the street bags so far."

"You want some coffee sweetie?"

The sharp knife of forgetfulness pierces my soul. I am no longer her sweetie. But, I can't attack her.

"Sure, milk and two sugars."

"I know."

"Great news guys. We made a big dent in the task. Six thousand packets of street-ready goods ready for sale. Henry Ford would be proud of our assembly line. We can work a while longer, finish the entire job, and leave tomorrow before noon. We will have ample time to get to Minneapolis. That way we won't have to worry about repackaging, transporting, and re-starting our work tomorrow. Everything will be done and ready. We can toss all the paraphernalia in the Dumpster behind the motel. That's the plan."

Back to our stations. The line is humming along only to be interrupted by the banging on the door.

"Bob. Open up it's me."

"Lazarus has risen."

"Maggie. Open up it's me."

To quiet him, Maggie rushes to the door and opens it enough for Tim to fall into the room. She catches him and leads him to the bed. The wind rushes in and causes a swirl at the table. The three of us instinctively lean over the powder to keep it from dusting the room. Some is blown into the floor carpet and the bed spreads. How did he find us?

"What are you doing?"

"Be quiet, Tim. We don't want any undo interference from neighbors or staff."

He whispers loudly in a mock tone like a petulant child.

"I want to do it too. Can I help?"

"Tim you're just in time for a nightcap. We've completed our work for the night. And we're all going to have a few drinks. What would you like? Some bourbon?"

"What's all that stuff on the table? I mean if you guys are done, what's all that doing just sitting there?"

"We're going to put it back in the bags and do some more work tomorrow. You can help us then. OK?"

"Yeah, bourbon. Jim Beam."

"Maggie, why don't you and Tim go back to your room? We'll meet you there in a few minutes. Then we can all have some drinks."

"OK. Upsy-daisy Tim. Let's go back to our room."

"You guys will be along real soon, eh?"

To prevent further loss of product, I hold a bed spread behind him as he exits. Hoisting and lugging a drunk is difficult. Performing these acts of heroism with someone whom is large, recalcitrant, and who smells foul is very difficult. Maggie is a trooper.

"Elaine. Jaqa. See you in five minutes. You need to stay here and continue to fill bags. I'll go to Maggie. We'll probably have to put a few drinks into Tim. He'll pass out and we'll be back to finish the task. Lock the door behind me."

Maggie answers the tapping. Her eyes are welled with tears. Not sure of the cause . . . humiliation, anger, or sadness.

"He's not quite passed out again. Let's give him a strong one. And do a lot of toasting. He'll be gone in fifteen minutes."

She pours. Tim gets three ounces. We get a taste and a lot of water. We toast the job. We toast Tariq. We toast our future. His glass falls from the edge of the bedside table and Tim falls back onto the pillow.

"Damn, smell. He puked on the bed. With the pee and vomit, the bed is nothing more than a giant smelly wet spot. I'll have to sleep on the floor."

"I'll take the mattress off the bed and put it on the floor. You can sleep on the box spring. It's dry."

"Why can't I stay with you tonight?"

"Because Tim will awaken, find you gone and raise a ruckus."

We lift Tim into the chair and make two half beds where there was once only one. We plop the sot.

"Asshole."

Maggie hisses as she closes the door and squeezes my hand. We return to the production line. Just like sex, motivated by completion, our activity is accelerated. The last bag is packed at 4:26 AM.

Great Friday

It's 10:30. I haven't slept this late in years. It disorients me. There is part of me that becomes anxious. I might have missed something by sleeping late. Something important may have happened that will impact my life and I was not there to experience it. Maybe it was nothing more that the sunrise. I'm alone in bed.

Packed and ready, we all meet at The Breakfaststop before getting back on the Interstate. Our booth is tucked away in the corner. There are only three other patrons. Tim shuffles to the table from the newsstand and telephones clutching *USA Today*.

"Who drugged me yesterday? I feel like shit."

"Tim, you had a short day. You partied with your buddy Jim Beam and slept soundly."

"Maggie, I'm sorry for messing the bed. But, I should get some points for separating the mattress and box spring so you didn't have to sleep in my mess."

"Right you are."

"Listen, I've had a bad time up to now. But, I'm better. You guys can count on me the rest of the way. By the way, check out the latest news from Albuquerque?"

DRUG DEAL LEADS TO SEVEN DEATHS

Albuquerque, New Mexico. State and local police, assisted by Federal agents, surmise that the bodies of four Mexican nationals and three mutilated Blacks are the result of a botched drug deal in the Grande Sierra housing development. As they sift through the carnage, police ask for help in identifying the two black men and a black woman, whose heads and hands were severed using the carpenter's band saw at the construction site. Police are seeking the cooperation of the Mexican Government in identifying the four Mexican men slain at the site.

"OK, we knew the cops would find the mess. It'll take them days to find the body parts that could lead to identifications. They will not look at the rest stop until someone notifies them. By then, they'll be unidentifiably rotten and we'll be long gone. But, we can't get lazy. We must push on. Today is a straight through. We can make the Twin Cities tonight. Our manufacturing is complete. I've got three rooms at TC MotorLodge on 114th Street and Pineway Boulevard. The rooms are being held for late arrival. All we have to do is get there. Elaine will contact Sharon this afternoon and the connection will be set. Let's switch the driving a little. Tim, you and I will ride with Maggie in the van. Contact is still limited to emergencies. OK? Let's make a movie."

Elaine takes my arm as we are leaving and whispers.

"Bob, when we finished, we were about half a kee short. Somewhere between all the scooping and Tim's untimely entrance, we lost half a kee. What should we do?"

"When you talk to Sharon, tell her we will deliver twenty-three and a half cut and four uncut."

The sun is bright and hot. The air is clean and clear. Winter's grip is about gone. All-in-all, a good driving day.

"Guys, I'm going to crash in the back. Wake me when it's my turn to drive."

His hangover, big breakfast, and the motion of the vehicle put Tim to sleep instantly. His snoring confirms the depth of his slumber.

"Now what?"

"We drive."

"I mean what do we do while we drive?"

"Camp songs are out of the question. I never went to camp. See what the radio has to offer, but keep it low. Conversation should be kept to whispers so as not to disturb sleeping pukie. The passenger can read, nap, or gaze. The drive, that's me for now, must pay attention to driving."

"Why worry about the asshole in the rear? He'll sleep until he is awakened. I'm not sure I can stand to be this close to you . . . alone in a van where no one can see us . . . without touching you. Running my hands over your thighs. Kissing you. Feeling you get excited."

"I'm almost there. Cut it out. Lest you forget our passenger, your husband; my charge, driving; and the confines of this vehicle, limited, anything beyond conversation between us is out of the question."

"Let me worry about all those big nasty details. You don't get it do you? Lover boy back there hasn't touched me in so long he is almost a stranger. That charade in the hot tub was my doing. His contribution was dry mouth and limp noodle. And now that he has revealed his true self as a weak incompetent, he repulses me. I deserve a strong man, a man who takes charge, a man who is focussed on success. I'm not old or ugly, and I have needs. And, without picking at a wound, given the recent coupling of Elaine and Jaqa, you must have needs, too. I know we'll be together after this is over. I gave you a taste of what was in store when we're together, now let me give you a thin slice of the sweet treat."

She takes my belt buckle in her left hand and fly zipper in her right. The angle of the zipper and its bends caused by my sitting, make her task of fly opening jerky. She perseveres. Her fingers find my shaft and extract it. She lowers her head to my lap and proceeds to flaunt her sexuality. Except Tim doesn't see her. I push the seat back to give her room. My mind wanders to Elaine and I start to compare. Maggie is better. Or, at least the situation is more erotic. Cars go by and haven't the foggiest idea what is going on. All they can see is a guy alone in a van. I have to avoid the big tucks and the RV's. Their height would give them a good perspective of what's going down. The speedometer now reads 55. I've lost concentration on driving and accelerate back up to 75. The sun has heated the air inside the vehicle. Or, is it just me?

Her hair is very fine and baby soft. Her shampoo is scented with sweet floral top notes of jasmine and gardenia and a warm base of cinnamon. Oldies from the 70's remind me of all the good times I've had and promise more of the same. Total sensory pleasure. She stops too early.

"See what I mean?"

"Why did you stop?"

"I told you I was going to give you a slice. I didn't say how big a slice."

The twinkle in her eyes and smile on her moist lips confirmed how coy she thought she was. I reach the back of her neck with my right hand and guide her head to its proper place. She offers no resistance. She needs me to take charge. I respond well to both of her games. Completion occurs at mile number 387. Rapture is problematic while driving 75 miles per hour. I have a strong urge to let go as I am letting go. After catching my breath and when my heart rate settles at 54, I zip my pants. The remainder of my turn at the wheel was boringly uneventful.

"Snow Bird. This is Black Bird. Do you copy?"

"Black Bird. This is Snow Bird. We copy."

"We're gonna take a stretch and break at rest stop number two. Care to join us?"

I shake my head.

"Black Bird. Not ready to swap out drivers. We'll push on to number three. Meet you at the motel. Thanks for the update."

"Now, how are you going to return the favor? How soon after I dump mister messy? Since it is I who is owed, I demand that you pay me in kind within two hours of my dumping the sultan of soil."

* *

The trip returns to tedium. Hills are becoming more noticeable. The farms are not as green. In fact, it looks as if some have not been plowed yet. But the road vehicles are the same. The drivers appear to be returning from winter in the South. My guess is all the states surrounding the Gulf, but mostly Florida. The real Snow Birds are coming home to their nests. Traffic thickens and is slowing ahead. The faint glimmer of brake lights indicates something is amiss.

"Snow Bird. This is Black Bird. Do you copy?"

"I copy, Black Bird. What's with this traffic?"

"Snow Bird. You are at the ass end of a semi-meets-RV pile up. It happened at the exit of rest stop two. We are stuck here until the mess is cleared. We can see at least two SUV's, three RV's, another semi, and assorted cars that have become entangled. Plus, there are numerous vehicles that wound up off the road as a result of bad braking. Chances are we'll be here for about an hour. The men at the gas station have already called the cops and have moved their wrecker onto the road. Where are you, Snow Bird?"

"Black Bird we are about five or six miles from the rest stop. The traffic is jamming behind us. I guess we'll be by the rest stop in 45 minutes. See you at the TC MotorLodge. Over."

"Now what?"

"We move when we can."

"If there is too much delay, we should stop at the rest stop."

"It will be a madhouse of cranky old farts with stressed colons and bladders. Once we get passed the rest stop, it will be clear and easy. Traffic will be thin and we can make up for lost time. Should we let Tim drive?"

"Let him sleep until we stop."

As our delay stretches, the gauges on the dash indicate the engine is heating. Can't pull off the road and lose our place in line. So, like many others, I just turn off the engine and wait for movement ahead. Some people even get out of their cars and seek vantage spots. Good idea. I climb out the window to the roof. Standing, I can see the three-lane serpent, but not its head. The sun and air refresh.

"Want some company?"

"Sure, Tim, come on up."

"Ah, man, what a mess. What the hell happened?"

"A semi played kissy-kissy with an RV. So we wait until they break."

"Hey, Bric . . . I mean Bob, when will we be cutting the smack?"

"Already done, Tim."

"Done without me?"

"You were occupied, by sleep."

"Sorry. Where are we?"

"Nearing our destination."

"I want to apologize for my behavior. I mean the drinking and not being there for you. I got fucked up, and now I'm paying for it. I feel like a large bag of dog shit sitting in the summer sun. But, my mind is straight now and I'm ready to carry my load. I've done OK so far, except for the booze, and I'll be there when you need me at the final deal."

"Tim, everything is under control. I know I'll need you at the final deal. And I know I can count on you being there when the chips are on the table."

"Hey, thanks man now I got to get straight with Marilee . . . I mean Maggie. I think she thinks I'm not holding up my end. A few soft words and some deep kisses will let her know the truth. I am the man. You going to stay up here?"

The jerk. He is truly wasted space. When he kisses Maggie, what will he taste? I stare into the fields. Why is farming so attractive to city people and something from which the young country folk wish to flee? I sit and ponder the universal truths of love and luck. The sun is hot in the air. I relax. My eyelids become heavy. The horn honking shatters the spell.

"Hey, man, the traffic is moving. Better get into the van. I'm about to head on down the road."

In through the side door and plop on the seat. Tim's face beams. He is contributing and thinks driving is atoning. We're back at it again. It's slow going at the accident site. We go from three lanes to one: from 15 to 5 miles per hour. We creep passed the recently created junkyard. Back up to highway speed.

"Elaine. See if you can reach the others."

"No can do. By now they're too far away."

＊ ＊

Settle in for the ride, and return to my pondering of rural versus city life. The combination pop and sploosh instantly precede the jerky motion of the vehicle as it veers toward the roadside.

"Hey, man what's happening. We're in trouble. I can't control the van."

Tim's whining is a fitting compliment to the car careening out of control. Having ignored the seatbelt law, the three of us bounce inside the compartment like lotto balls. I slam against the front seat. Maggie smacks her head against the dash, but rights herself immediately. Tim grips the wheel and it turns his hands. Maggie and I have nothing to grip. The van turns sideways. First to the right, then to the left. I slide from one side of the bench seat to the other. Smashing against the interior walls. My arms, knees and ribs get smacked.

Maggie is bouncing around like Raggedy Ann. Her upper body and arms seem to strike every available surface; dash, door, and inner roof. During my famous back seat trampoline act, I see blood oozing from her nose and the mark on her forehead. The softness of the earth accelerates the deceleration. At our stop we are at an angle to the road. Maggie is crumpled on the floor.

"What the fuck happened, man?"

"Tim, check Maggie. I'll check the tires."

Sliding the door open is an ordeal. The front left tire is in shreds, and the rim is bent.

"Bric, come here quick."

I guess he'll never learn.

"She looks really hurt. Let's get her out of the van. Slowly. Carefully."

She is pale and her face is covered with blood. After thirty seconds, she slowly blinks her eyes open.

"Honey where does it hurt?"

No response. She looks at Tim and me

"Are you OK? Where does it hurt?"

"All over. Too numb to tell where all the pain is coming from specifically. Can't move my left arm at all. I need to catch my breath. Need to rest. Shit, I really hurt."

"We need to get her to a hospital. She could be seriously injured. You know internal damage."

"Tim, let's give her a few moments. Get clothes from the bags. Keep her warm and comfortable. Maggie, just relax. You took a big bump to your forehead. How's your vision? I mean, can you focus?"

"A little blurry. You guys are going in and out of focus."

As cars roar by, we rig a roadside rest bed for her. Breathing is painful for me. Bruised rib or ribs. Tim takes care of the tire. We must have picked up a piece of glass or metal from the accident. The third fuck up on Tim's watch. No more. The spare is beneath a panel in the back compartment. It takes him ten minutes to get it and the jack and then another twenty minutes before the van has four good shoes. The man is dangerous and slow.

"What are we going to do for her? We have to get her to a hospital. X-rays and stuff."

"If we take Maggie to a hospital now, there are going to be too many questions that we can't answer. Plus, we'll lose a day. We can't afford the questions or to lose the time."

"Bob's right. I can manage for a while. After we do the final deal, I can ask Elaine's friend, Sharon, for the name of a

Doctor, who is off the books, and needs cash. Or a clinic that treats the low life who want to avoid public records. I've got some heavy-duty pain pills in my bag. Get them for me. Now. And one of the pops in the back. I'll live with the pills for a day or two. But, I am pretty sure my left arm is broken. Can you rig a sling?"

"Honey, I am sure you should have your injuries looked after right away."

"Listen, fuck-up, since these are my injuries, I'll determine when they should be examined and by whom. I don't want to do anything that could queer the deal. So, do as I tell you. Get my pills, rig a sling, and move me to the back of the van. I need my rest."

The line was drawn. Tim on the outside, Maggie on the inside. For now, in the eyes of the general public, I am Swiss.

"Maggie, this is going to sound weird, but I need you to cough up some spit. You can tell by the pain when you cough, if you sustained broken ribs, and we can tell by the color of the mucus if there is lung or throat damage."

The contortion in her face and the impulsive doubling over corroborate the intensity of the pain. But, the luggie is big and milky colored. Nothing damaged in her lungs. At least not that I can see so far. No way to know about other internal organs without a full exam. I'm a little worried about the damage done by the blows to her head. Better keep an eye on that. Check her urine at the next stop. We pull back into traffic. It's interesting that no one stopped to see if we were all right or needed help. So much for the concept of the Good Samaritan.

The next hour is spent in silence until Tim turns on the radio. No one speaks for another hour.

"Baby, up ahead is a rest stop. We'll go in there for a stretch and a john visit. Are you OK? Can you get out of the van?"

"I don't hurt nearly as much as I did a while back. These pills are good. But, I need to walk around a bit just to make sure everything functions properly. Uhghgh."

"What's the matter?"

"I just rolled over on my side and I hurt. Ribs, arm, and knees. But, I'll be OK. Pull into the rest stop."

Getting Maggie from the back of the van is slow. She grits her teeth in pain. She is a real trooper. Walking to the main building and the restrooms, her steps are measured and sometimes she staggers. She has cleaned most of the blood from her face, but the puffiness and redness at the impact point is unmistakable. Her sling works. She heads for the ladies' room promising to check her functions. I head for the men's room. Then coffee. Tim buys a tire from the service station. After thirty minutes, he is ready. Why so long? No Maggie. Time drags as anxiety builds.

"Where is she, man"?

The whiner is back with a vengeance.

"Women always take more time in the can than men do. And, I'm sure she is slowed by her injuries. We'll give her another ten minutes. If she doesn't show, you'll have to go and get her. We have to keep her condition to the three of us.

From the door to the ladies' room shuffles Maggie. She is ashen and her pace is obviously labored.

"Let's get out of here now. Help me to the van quickly. Hold on tight."

On the road again.

"I hate to be clinical, but what happened in there?"

"I coughed and it hurt like hell. No blood though. My urine is like tea. That may be blood. But I saw no spots on the paper. The bad news is that I am very dizzy. I see spots if I move my head rapidly. I can't get a sharp focus on anything small like words on a page. And everything sounds dull and distant, as if I had a thick wool blanket wrapped around my head. I am afraid I've a concussion along with my broken arm and ribs. I'm gonna' have to see a doctor as soon as we get to Minneapolis. I'm not sure the codeine I'm taking is not affecting my head. And it sure knots up my stomach."

"Baby, I'll get us to the Twin Cities chop-chop."

"Maggie, if Tim drives like *el speedo*, in a short time, we'll be able to contact Elaine. I'll tell her about the situation. She can contact Sharon on a landline. Sharon can direct us to the right place to have you checked out. Hang in there."

"Yeah, baby, hang in there. We'll get you fixed up chop-chop."

Tim pushes the van to 85. Maggie's condition is not good. This is bad. What to do with a wounded soldier? Medic, morgue or Minneapolis?

* *

Sharon will meet us at the ER as close to ten as we can make it. She'll shepherd us through the paper work, nosey nurses, and miscreants. I will accompany Maggie. By the time we get to the Twin Cities, Tim is ranting like it was his head that got smacked. I leave him with the two lovers. I have cash. Park the van and walk Maggie to the sliding doors.

The hubbub and antiseptic smell slap me. At the reception desk, I sign in . . . only six ahead of us. I get a clipboard, admitting form, and a pen. While Maggie slumps beside me and stares like she is on heavy doses of thorazine, I complete the minutia boxes. Just enough information to receive care. Not enough to get us traced.

"Excuse me, sir, are you Bob Welch?"

Our goddess of the rapid recovery is blonde, blue eyed, and looks about thirty.

"Yes, and you are . . ."

"Sharon Fallon. I'm here to help you. Is this Maggie Conrad?"

"Yes, she . . . ."

"If you've completed the form, I'll take Maggie to an examining room."

"I would like to be with her as much as possible"

"I understand. Let's go to the elevator."

"But, aren't the ER examining rooms on his floor."?

"Yes, they are. Here give me the form and clipboard. I'll drop them at the desk."

She deposits the clipboard and pen on the desk and takes the form with her. Elevator rides in hospitals are slow. Sharon crumples the form and stuffs it into a pocket.

"Were your told about payment? Cash. Five hundred for me and one thousand for the doctor, who will examine your friend. There will be no charge for the room. Or any tests or medications your friend needs. Is this clear?"

"Clear."

Sharon takes the five bills and stuffs them in her bra. The hall is dim. At the nurses station sit two nearly comatose human monitors. The sign on the wall reads *Oncology*. The death ward. Everyone is sleeping for now. A few for the last time. The nurses don't look up from their paperbacks. We enter room 541.

"The doctor will be here in a few minutes. In the meantime, your friend should get onto the bed."

Sharon's eyes are cold and empty like a shark's, and her voice has all the warmth of a mortician. But, she's all we have. Despite his beard, the doctor looks like he is about sixteen. He is costumed in the appropriate manner; long white coat, stethoscope draped around his neck, glasses and a pocket protector with some drug company's name. No nametag.

"Is this Ms. Conrad?"

"Yes."

"And you are . . ."

"Her friend."

"Fine. Payment is due in advance."

I count out ten one hundreds, and he stuffs them in his right pant's pocket.

"Now, Ms. Conrad. Tell me what happened."

As she whispers, he touches her abdomen, puts the stethoscope to her chest, and then moves her arms and legs. Her pain is obvious. He spends a good amount of time on her head. He peers into eyes with a pin flashlight. Maggie looks left, right, up, and down.

"I can get the arm into a temporary splint. It will be adequate for a few days. You'll have to come back or go to a clinic . . . I can give you the name of a suitable doctor . . . to have the arm set for the long haul. If you can give me a urine sample, I'll look at it. There doesn't seem to be any palpable organ damage. An X-ray would give me more information. We can do that here; on this floor . . . it'll take about ten minutes. I can tape the ribs. That's the only thing that will help. At the same we're getting a look at your torso, I'll get a quick peak at your head. Unfortunately, a quick peak will only expose any major issues.

Minor issues can only be determined by a complete CAT scan. That takes an appointment and an admitting physician. However, as of now I don't think the CAT scan will be necessary. I'm also going to give you some antibiotics, a muscle relaxant, and pain pills that are just as strong as codiene, but easier on your system. Please eat while your are taking these medications. Nothing fatty. Nothing fried. For a few days limit your diet to breads, herbal tea, banana's, tuna, steamed vegetables and broiled chicken. No alcohol. And lots of rest. You must monitor your urine for any dark precipitation, your stools for black discoloration, and your mucus for dark spots. These are all indications of blood, and should be considered warning signs that something severe is amiss. If you note blood, you must be see a doctor or come back to this hospital. We will walk you down to the X-ray room at the end of the hall. Sir, you may come along if you wish."

The doctor has a strange way of pointing. The index finger of his right hand is crooked into the web between his thumb and palm, and he points with his middle, ring and pinky finger as a unit. Maggie pees in a beaker and hands it to the good doctor. He shines a bright light behind the beaker, swirls the contents, and stares at the liquid. Smiling, he nods his head. I don't notice any precipitation. But, what the hell do I know.

I help her remove her pull over and bra. She has almost perfectly formed firm breasts. The doctor wraps tape up and down and around the rib cage. I help her return the pull over. No room for the bra. The four of us navigate the hall. Doors on either side are partially open. Glances reveal men and women in suspended animation with tubes running from them to pumps, drips and monitors. When is it time to pull the plug?

According to the doctor, the X-rays of both torso and Maggie's head reveal no rips, punctures, breaks, or cracks. The film, beaker, and bra are tossed down a waste shoot. She is good to go. Exit is slow, but easy. She sits in the passenger seat.

"How you doin'?"

"Much better. I'm tired, but relieved that I didn't do any more damage than we had suspected. I'll go to the clinic and have my arm set after the deal. Let's get it done in a hurry. I want to get to my new life now."

SATURDAY NIGHT DANCE

The TC MotorLodge is like thousands of older big city economy motels . . . the ones built between the fringe of "downtown" and the suburbs 30 years ago. Twenty years later urban renewal followed the same major road toward the 'burbs, but leap-frogged some neighborhoods, which have deteriorated into a combination of sleazy almost-transient motels, warehouses, and small shops. The buildings could use a thorough steam cleaning, two coats of paint and all new windows. The city street sweepers make infrequent visits. The nice thing about the place and the neighborhood is that nobody seems to notice our arrival. Three rooms. Two nights. Paid in cash up front.

Maggie's job is to get better. This means rest and care. Tim's job is to care for her. This means sobriety and attentiveness. Elaine's job is to set the meeting. This means contact with Sharon . . . not the other way. So, Elaine has to drive a few miles to use different payphones. Jaqa's job is to kvetch. This means she is in contact with all of us, all the time. My job is to plan. The place of the purchase, the arrival, the transaction, departure, and final departure. All stages of the main event must be analyzed from diverse perspectives. We are not going to the local bank and taking out a car loan. We are selling drugs to criminals for a lot of money. I have already seen that if anything can go wrong it will. Murphy was a prophet. Scribble notes on 3 x 5 cards, which will be burned before the meeting. Extraneous issues flood my mind. How to care for Maggie? What to do about Tim? How I feel about Elaine? How to avoid Jaqa?

"Bob, we need to talk about my husband's share of the money. He would be looking at something in the neighborhood of 250 grand. As a couple that meant a half a million. That's a much nicer neighborhood than this one. Because Omar . . . Tariq . . . was my husband, I'm entitled to his share. It's only right."

"Jaqa, at the beginning, we agreed to divide the final cash into equal shares. Then there were six, now there are five. I told you in Albuquerque that Tariq's share would remain in the pot. Therefore, when this is over, each of us will receive one-fifth of the reward."

"Who made you boss?"

"I did. I've lead this expedition from the beginning. You were happy when I was making decisions that were agreeable to you. Now you're not happy, because you've gotten greedy."

"The way I heard it, it was Tim's idea from the beginning. You just stole his thunder. I say we put it to a vote among all five of us. Majority rules. Fair?"

"Tim hasn't had an original idea in his life. This entire venture would have never gotten off the ground if it weren't for me. And, fair is not an issue. You are putting self-interest above the interests of the group. Greed above agreement. Just because the situation has changed, you want to change the agreement. Your self-serving point-of-view does not warrant a group discussion."

"Elaine feels as I do. So, it's not just my point-of-view."

"Of course your lover would feel the same. She stands to benefit from the grab-as-grab-can approach. So her opinion is not even remotely objective. I'm sure Tim and Maggie would agree with the concept of share and share alike. They knew the agreement at the beginning. And, they must believe it's the same now."

"He was my husband and that's my money. Period."

"He was your soon-to-be ex-husband and you will receive one-fifth of what would have been his share. Period. Now please leave me alone, I have a lot to do."

The door slamming was only less annoying than her carping, just more emphatic. When she was upset or felt threatened, her voice was reminiscent of fingernails on the blackboard. How quickly I had forgotten this trait so necessary in our telephone days. She even slammed the door to her room. Back to planning. Do I return Tim's gun? What did Ahmed teach about the meeting procedure? What would the other guys do to get an edge? What must I do to anticipate this action and nullify it? It's different. Now, I have to worry about a third force . . . the police.

Maybe they let a few dealers alone to use them as bait just for people like us. Maybe the cops have bugged Sharon's place. Are they following her, too? Who else knows? If we meet in an open, yet private place, the out-of-towners are vulnerable to ambush. If we meet in a well-populated place, the risk of gunfire, at least from the cops, is eliminated. But, the cops can watch, record, and follow us. Meet briefly in one place and deal at another very shortly after the meeting. Just like Ahmed. Meet in public and deal in private after all the loose ends are tied off.

Can't afford a repeat of Albuquerque. Got to do something to control Tim. Keep him calm. Not booze. The shit in the bag. He'll never shoot up. Take the partial and give him some to snort. That procedure is not foreign to him. No, that would jeopardize the upcoming events and cut into our cash reward. Also, favoritism would be a bargaining chip to the two dykes. If, Tim, why not Jaqa? Right on cue, they are knocking on the door.

"Bob, honey, we need to talk."

The preface to a heated argument is no different when she was my lover or now as my ex. I should ask her to drop the honey. But, why bother?

"Sure come on in."

"Now what's this visit all about?"

"It's about my late husband's share of the money."

"You mean the man you recently left for the arms of my ex-lover. Listen, let's get all the players and the titles straight . . . oops bad choice of words."

"Sweetie, there's no reason to be bitchy."

"Elaine, I am no longer your sweetie or your honey. I am the leader of this group of criminals, who take from the low, deal to the lower, and profit the riches. Whatever was is past?"

"OK, Bob, then be reasonable. Jaqa is entitled to the share that would have gone to her husband."

"No."

Normally, when I deal with some one in an acrimonious or adversarial situation, the more direct my questions and more terse my responses to their questions, the stronger my position is and the more likely I will prevail. It's like dealing with the cops or an attorney. K.I.S.S. rules.

"I think all of us should discuss this matter."

"Can't Jaqa speak for herself or are you two so close that you think and feel as one? Or, did you convince her that you could convince me to change my position? While I appreciate your offer of unbalanced distribution, I must decline the considered invitation."

Another ploy in negotiating is to treat the opposition's position as a kindly, yet trivial offer. This minimizes its importance so that it can be dismissed with politeness. Elaine has seen this before and it really pisses her off.

"Enough of your shit. We demand a vote of the team. Let the team decide."

"Thanks, but no thanks. Is that it?"

"No. That's not it? We want Jaqa's money."

"Now, it's we want her money. Convenient covetousness. First she wants what is not hers, then you want your piece of what is not yours. Greed does not become either of you."

"Jaqa, get Tim and bring him here. We'll vote."

"Ladies, as it were, if you insist on going through with this doomed power play, why don't we all go to Tim and Maggie's room so that all five of us can discuss this. Let the other people see your avarice."

Hoping for a female/male split of the vote, they nearly sprint to the other room. Elaine knocks resolutely.

"Hello, who is it?"

"Tim, it's all of us, we need to discuss something of the utmost importance."

We enter the ersatz recovery room.

"Sit where you can, Maggie's just finished her lunch. She can have visitors for only a short time. Then she must rest."

"Hi girl, how you feelin'?"

"Well enough given what I went through. I can control the pain and I'm getting used to taking shallow breaths."

"That's great. We won't be but a minute. It seems that our fearless leader has decided that I am not entitled to receive what is rightfully mine. By that I mean my late husband's share of the money. Bob has agreed that we should discuss this matter and put it to a vote among the entire group."

Good ploy. Putting their position for a vote in my mouth. They hope this will confuse Tim and Maggie. Now, I can't deny that position. So I must go along with it.

"My point-of-view is that we entered into this episode on the basis for equal share for everybody. Jaqa's then husband accepted this, as did we all. Now he is dead. Now there are only five parties to share in the loot. I feel strongly that each of us should receive one-fifth. Jaqa believes that she should receive two-sixths and each of us should get only one sixth of the total.

Let's assume that we can sell all the kees for a grand total of two million. If we each get one-fifth we get 400 grand, whereas Jaqa feels she should get 800 grand and each of us should get 300 grand. The question is should one of us, regardless of who, receive more than twice what the others receive, or should we all get equal slices of the cake? It's as simple as that. And, because the matter involves a large amount of cash, I did not feel I should be the one to make the decision for everybody."

I twist their ploy to make me the hero of team play.

"Jaqa, I thought all along that we would share equally in the money. Bob was right to ask us all. I want my equal slice. Tim?"

Did I notice Maggie wink at me?

"I agree with Maggie."

"Then it's settled. Three to two in favor of equal shares. Case closed. Elaine, when do you call Sharon to confirm the meeting?"

The two froze their facial muscles in rage.

"In about thirty minutes."

"I'll go with you to make the phone call.

"Hey, Bob could you sit with Maggie, while I go out for while. I want to drive out to a mall and get something special for my girl. It's her birthday tomorrow."

"Sure, Tim. After we learn about the time and place, stop somewhere and get a sponge cake and maybe some sorbet. We should have a party for the birthday girl. Tomorrow will be too hectic."

Two cars. Two directions.

* *

"Maggie, how do you feel? Imagine I'm your doctor and I need as much detail as possible."

"Have not coughed so I haven't coughed up anything. No dark precipitate in my pee. Have not moved my bowels so that precinct has yet to report in. The pain pills have constipated me. If I breathe shallow, there is not much pain. My arm hurts like a mother, when I accidentally move or bump it. It throbs big time right at the spot of the swelling. I have to get it set in two days . . . three days at the latest. My vision is still fuzzy, and I get dizzy if I move my head suddenly.

My nose hurts. Raccoon rings are starting to appear at my eyes. The lump on my forehead throbs. The pain pills work for the most part, and the muscle relaxants are marvelous. I double dosed once and got so loosey-goosey that Tim looked fuckable. Don't want to make that mistake again. How's that doc? Do you want me to remove all my clothes so that you can examine me thoroughly?"

"That would be a violation of the AMA code of ethics. Now, how have you slept?"

"Soundly, once I can close my eyes and the room stops swirling. This goes away in a few minutes. Then I'm fine except when I roll over on my arm. Other than the dizziness, I feel much better. I should be able to ride old paint away from the sheriff."

"Great. The day after, we'll get you to a doctor. Now rest. That's this doctor's orders. I'll sit with you until Tim returns. If you need anything just ask."

"I did and you said no."

"That was a situational response. What I meant was not now."

She fell asleep after ten minutes of some local schlock show. Today it was children who have children with older people. The first couple was a guy, who claimed to be 65 and his lover, who claimed to be 16. They were paired with a 61 year-old woman and a 17 year-old boy. After the second commercial break, the teens were giving each other the lust look. My eyelids get heavy.

* *

"Wake up you, two. It's time to eat sweet treats, and for the birthday girl to open her presents."

The cheery threesome bounds into the room. My deep sleep causes disorientation. My 3 x 5 cards spill onto the floor. I have to scoop them up and put them in order. Maggie is startled awake. Her eyes are wide open and they blink like an owl.

"Guys, I'll be right back."

Throwing the sheet and blanket aside, Maggie leaps to the bathroom. I note two small dark spots on the bottom sheet, where her butt rested. She yells from the bathroom.

"That explains it."

"What?"

"My monthly friend has come to visit. I wondered why I felt so full, when I hadn't eaten much. I was beginning to worry. But, I'm bloated. Now, I crave sugar. Bring on the sweets for the birthday girl."

Conviviality returns to the group. Elaine and Jaqa bought little party favors for all. Plus, a nightgown for Maggie. Tim bought her some perfume and the latest novel by John Andes. Mercifully, the daytime TV trash was extinguished.

"Sharon says she will have the money by tomorrow at night. We can meet either at ten or early the morning of the day after. I thought it would be better to meet at night and leave the area."

"Perfect. Where does she want to do the deal?"

"I'm to call her again to confirm the place."

"Elaine, I'm not crazy about so damned many contacts. If anybody is listening to her phone, they'll know for sure something big is going to happen. If it's the DEA, we're in for a short night and a long slow life."

Suddenly everyone got quiet and looked worried.

"If you guys thought this part of the whole deal was clean and pure, you weren't thinking straight. Look at the facts. Here is a dealer, Sharon, who was left untouched by the cops when they swept the city. You gotta believe they know about her. My bet is that they are watching her to pick up any scraps they left behind. She is a Judas goat, who leads others to slaughter. But, because we know this, we can plan accordingly. Sharon will set the meeting place. We will show up. Well, not all of us.

Elaine and I will show up. You three will be at a second location. We will explain to Sharon that the deal will be done elsewhere at a place of our choosing. Sharon, Elaine, and I will drive in one car to the new place. She can have her people deliver the stuff there. I'm sure they all use cell phones. This way her people can't ambush us. If the cops are on her butt, we'll see them follow us to the second location. Then we split. Fuck the deal. Fuck the money. We have currency of a special realm. If no one follows us, we make the trade. Smack for cash. I have this all worked out."

"Listen, I called Sharon at the hospital. No phone taps there. So not to worry scaredie cat. I'm not sure your plan is all that good. It's right out of Ahmed's handbook. It worked so well the last time, why not try it again. Hell, we only lost three at the purchase. With any kind of luck we'll only lose two this time."

"Thanks for the vote of confidence, Elaine, dearest. Let's not be mired in history. Mine, yours, or ours. If you have an idea, any idea in your head will do, let us have it. Otherwise, shut the fuck up."

Silence floods the room.

"Where is the second location?"

"I have three possibilities in mind and want to scout them tonight. I'll make the final determination after my excursion."

"Then we'll all know?"

"Yes, then we'll all know. What's the big deal? I've planned this thing damned well so far. Haven't I? I'll let you know when I know. Does Sharon know what we have in street-ready packets and that we have many bags of uncut merchandise ready to break down?"

"She knows."

"Did you discuss price?"

"She'll do an on-site test. If it's as good as we say, she'll pay the amount we ask. If the stuff is inferior, she'll pay between one million and a million five."

"That tells me she will bring less than a million five, because she plans to short us. She'll tell us the stuff is inferior and that it's worth much less that we had hoped. She'll say this regardless of how it checks out. OK, I can deal with her, because I am going to bring my own tester. If you all will excuse me, I need a nap before my late night trip."

* *

In my room, I turn on the early news. It's four fifteen.

"This just in from NewsBreaker 9 Mobile Unit 2 reporting from the Minneapolis-Saint Paul International airport. Our on-the-scene team is with the police, who have just uncovered substantial evidence in the Duluth armored truck robbery. Let's go live to Megan O'Malley."

"Brendan, we are standing in front of the car the police confirm was involved in the robbery of an armored truck in Duluth last week. The armored truck robbery that netted $65,000. Just moments ago, the police opened the trunk of the car and discovered three sets of jumps suits, gloves, and masks, along with what appear to be the checks, small bills, and change

from the robbery, further confirmed by the fact that these items were in bags marked with the name of various retail operations in Duluth. The police are getting ready to haul the vehicle away for further analysis at the police lab. I have with me, Lieutenant Bregson. Lieutenant, just how did you come to discover the get away car?"

"The airport police had been advised by our department to be on the look out for any suspicious vehicles. This one had been parked here for a while, so in their routine process, they examined it. They noticed the serial numbers, normally visible by the driver's side of the windshield, had been removed. That is a crime in and of itself. They notified us. We came out, popped the driver's door and then the trunk. That's when we found the evidence, which is now on the way to our lab for detailed analysis. This is a hot lead and gives us reason to believe we can follow the criminals out-of-state. The fact that the airport police uncovered the car is an example of fine interagency cooperation. All members of the investigative force are working long and hard to track the killers from this point. Remember, they are killers."

"Thank you Lieutenant Bregson. That's it for now. We will follow this story down at the police lab. From the airport this is Megan O'Malley for NewsBreaker 9."

Well they are only one week behind us. We're leading them by their noses. Sixty-five thousand? Bull shit. The little shops would be honest in their reporting, but *Nooners* must not want the world to know how much cash they take in over a big weekend. No sense in advertising how lucrative the saloon business really is. Somebody may think about robbing the place. Now I need a nap.

* *

First possibility is the parking lot of the Northgate Mall. Lots of space and exits. Video cameras for customer security. Nowhere to put microphones. But ample hiding places for snipers. Deal will take about twenty minutes to conclude. Can we get it done in time to avoid detection by a passing sector squad car? A drive by could happen, so it will. Next is the main parking lot of Hennipan Community College. No students at the time of the trade. Campus cops are lazy. They'll see what appear to be students' cars so they'll stay away. The lighting is bad. Exits are good. Straight shot to the interstate. But, main roads around the campus are ideal for general police patrol during the night.

Third possibility is the War Memorial Park just east of downtown. Dark. Easy access. Not populated at our hour. But, home to our ultimate clientele. Therefore, too many plain-clothes cops. Decisions. Decisions. Decisions. Back to the palace of poverty. The tension between Elaine and me is becoming tactile.

Somewhere between the strange image of sloping hills and noon, Elaine calls to announce that the deal is set for the hospital-parking garage at ten. No guards and only minor traffic, so we'll blend in. Now we wait. And wait and wait.

* *

"Maggie, how you feelin'?"

"Shitty, real shitty. Let's get this damned thing over with. My arm is really swollen and I'm getting dizzier. Can't focus on anything and motion makes me want to puke. But, the pain pills and the relaxants are wonderful."

"Where's Tim?"

"Who the fuck knows."

"When he just wanders off I get concerned."

"He's no threat to us."

"I'm not worried about us, I'm worried about his ability to screw up the deal. He's got a perfect record, three-for-three. Maybe I'm just getting paranoid. I have to go out for a while to confirm our departure. We'll need a new vehicle. Something with a little more punch than a van. And a lot sexier to match our new 'tudes. By the way, we never discussed where we should go. Where do you want to relocate?"

"I was thinking someplace warm. Maybe Texas or Florida. A small town. Maybe rural. A farm house. What about you?"

"A farm house sounds great. Somewhere cheap. Where they don't ask a lot of questions. We need the money to last until we can blend into the society and get jobs. Let's try Texas."

"Sounds good to me. Where?"

"South Texas near the Gulf. Outside of Brownsville. Farm and the beach . . . a great combination. I should be back before sunset. Rest easy."

First stop Viking Travel Services. Two tickets from O'Hare to Dallas for cash. Second stop Northland Motors. Trade-in the van for a three-year old Mustang. The sleaze bag didn't use KY or kiss me when the whole thing was over. But, he loved cash and asked no questions. Third stop, West End Luggage and Leather. I was on the next leg of the race.

Maggie looks like shit. She's pale and sweating as she sleeps. Tim is asleep in the chair beside her.

THE DAY OF REST

I can't recall if the expression is *No rest for the wicked* or *No rest for the weary.* In either case there will be no rest until the day is done. It's eight o'clock and time for a final walk through. We're ready to rock and roll.

"Elaine and I will meet Sharon at the garage."

"Tim, you, Jaqa, and Maggie will be at the Hennipan Community College main parking lot. Go to Row T, and park facing the exit. We will arrive about eleven. If you see any other cars or notice anybody moving around other than an occasional campus guard, radio us and we will abort. Got that."

"Got it. Do you think Maggie is OK to travel."?

"No, Tim, I think we should abandon her here. That was a stupid question."

"What I'm saying is should we take her to a hospital ER and leave her for treatment."

"Loose ends Tim, loose ends. One loose end and the cardigan unravels. If we leave her, she becomes an avenue to us for the police. She'll be fine, until we can get her some serious treatment. Tomorrow for sure. Now, everybody pack and load the cars. I'll check us out of the rooms."

The two ladies leave. Tim is at the door.

"Tim, wait. I have a change in plans for us. Not them. Just you and me. We won't be meeting at the Community College. We'll come back here to make the deal. We'll do it in my room."

"But you just said . . ."

"I know what I just said. I just told Elaine what I wanted her to tell Sharon."

"What?"

"Look, I trust me, you, and Maggie. Elaine and Jaqa have decided to go their own way. I have this odd feeling that Elaine and Sharon have discussed more than Elaine has told me. I fear that Sharon is a modern day Judas Goat. This is what I want you to do. When we leave in our separate cars, you head for the CC. When we meet Sharon, she'll test the merchandise. Then we'll haggle over price. As we are leaving the garage, I'll notify you. At that point you leave the CC parking lot and return to the motel. If you're followed let me know right away. We'll queer the deal and split."

"You'll call me. Any code?

"Yes, *the elves have left the building*. When you hear that, you'll know we're heading back to the motel. If there is a problem at your end, let me know. Otherwise, just stay off the air and meet me back here. Got that."

"Got it. What do we do about Sharon if there is a mess at my end?"

"I'll take care of Sharon. Don't worry about that. You just get the fuck away with the stuff. Take all the turns on all the streets you can. Avoid and evade. We'll wait for you on the Interstate heading West. And be careful with Maggie. She's very weak."

"I'll go to the CC and wait for your call. If all is fine at my end, I'll meet you back here. If there is a screw up, I'll flee. Can do? How about if there is a screw up, you and I meet at the train station? It's in a real seedy part of town. I've been there before. It'll be safe from whoever is following me. Better than waiting in the pen on the Interstate. Then we can leave town."

"Train station it is."

He grabs two anodized cases. And heads for the ladies. I get the three handguns. Tim's still wrapped in a carpenter's rag. No need to keep it clean now. I take two pieces each with full clips and a third clip with ten rounds. Put the third gun with a full clip in my jacket.

"Are you ready, Elaine?"

"Ready to get this mess over with."

"It's not over yet. So be alert and careful."

Tim and Jaqa guide Maggie into the back of the Chevy and she disappears onto the seat. They leave for the CC. Elaine slumps in passenger seat. Petulant child. We head for our meeting with Sharon.

"After the deal, we go our separate ways. Have you and Jaqa decided where you're going?"

"Quito, Ecuador."

"Ecuador?"

"Yeah, it's cheap and far away. Jaqa suggested it. We can get there by plane, boat, and plane. No one will be able to follow us. Jaqa and I can paint. She's really quite good, although you'd never know it. Tariq stifled her expression. When they were married, she hid her work. She's taught me so much about expression through that medium. I owe my outing to her. And you?"

"Not absolutely sure. I'll probably head for the mountains. Montana or Idaho. Settle in a small town. Get a job at some store. Start over."

"What about Tim and Maggie?"

"I understand they plan to head south. Florida."

"Look, I want you to know I never meant to hurt you. Life just happened. One minute I thought I was a straight female, the next I knew I was gay. It was nothing you did or didn't do. It was and is all about me. I've done a lot of reviewing of my past and I can see times when I was attracted to other women, but sat on the feelings. They were inappropriate, and definitely inconvenient. It's not that my relationships with men were wrong or evil; it's just that they were not complete. My job gave me some satisfaction.

Sure I wanted to run the ER, but I knew a nurse would never get that position. I had risen to the top in a small world. Our life was good, but there was this emptiness. Emptiness that you or we couldn't fill. Then I found Jaqa, and my life became more than I had thought possible. Thoughts, expressions, emotions . . . all buried were coming to life. I felt complete. Does that make sense to you?"

"Yes, but it still hurts. What the fuck it's in the past. We each have separate futures. Lives we want. So, let's take them with no looking back."

"Thanks for understanding, sweetie."

The verbal knife again. This time spoken with no feeling. Her rote response told me what I didn't want hammered into my heart. Except for road noise, the rest of the drive is silent.

✳ ✳

The hospital garage is a four-story monster covering two city blocks. There are signs everywhere to write your specific parking spot, so you can find your car after your visit. The first floor is reserved for handicapped drivers and doctors. That may be redundant. The nurses and other personnel fend for space on the second floor. Floors three and four and the roof are reserved for visitors. There is an enclosed walk way from the fourth floor to the hospital.

"Go to the fourth floor, and look for space 435-D."

"Easy enough. We're early by about ten minutes."

Space 435-D is surrounded by dark emptiness. There isn't a car within six spaces on in all directions. It is the island of void in a sea of cars. The lights, which seem to run in ribbons across the ceiling, are strangely non-functional above and around the spot. The tubes are in their places. They're just not lighted. A perfect place for an ambush. Eerie. We park with the engine running. Our car is pointed toward the exit. We wait in silence.

Waiting can lull into distraction or sharpen the senses to danger. In ten minutes I am so paranoid I can hear dirt as it's swept along the floor by the breeze. Two sets of running lights approach. One set belongs to a sedan, the other a pickup. The pickup is jacked. The frame and body are nearly a foot above normal. The two vehicles stop to the right and left behind my 'Stang.

"Don't get out of the car until one of them does."

"But, I want Sharon to see me and know its safe."

"Safety is my main concern. Ours not theirs."

The pickup flashes its lights three times. I tap my brake lights thrice. The passenger side door of the pickup opens and out slithers a shape, which is vaguely familiar. First one foot on the step bar. Then the second. The first foot on the floor. Then the second. Door is closed, but not shut. Khaki pants, boots, white T-shirt, and a dark baseball cap with no insignia. Facial hair. The character stands by the truck cab and waits. High beam lights from the truck and the sedan illuminate the previously dark ring. Into the now lighted ring steps the stranger.

"Now?"

"Now, but slowly."

"Sharon, it's me, Ellie. Hey, you're not Sharon. Where is she? Who are you?"

"I'm a friend of Sharon's. She sent me to consummate the deal."

My turn. I exit the car.

"Sorry, friend, we only do business with Sharon."

"I will conduct business with you."

"Wrong. No Sharon. No business. And we are ready to deal. What a shame. Where is Sharon?"

"Wait here a minute."

The vaguely familiar stranger removes his cap. Above his head he waves the cap twice. A third set of running lights approaches from the front and stops about twenty feet from my car. High beams are hit immediately upon stopping. The driver's door of a dark Mercedes SL400 Convertible opens and out steps a female version of the stranger. Her curves are my clues. Sharon is in the appropriate spotlight as she strides with purpose, yet stealthy grace toward the 'Stang.

"Hey, Ellie, how you doin'?"

"Sharon, it's good to see you."

"Shall we close the deal and move on? Before I put up cash, I want to check the quality of the merchandise."

"I have some for you to sample."

"And you are?"

"I am Bob. This is my party. Welcome."

"Well, Bob, I guess you and I are about to open the piñata. If your stuff is righteous, you win a lot of money. But, I determine righteous from almost righteous. And that determines how much money you get, Bob."

She pops the first and last letters of my name and gives the three-letter name two syllables. It sounds like an evil chant. I mimic her by elongating the *sh* sound and emphasizing both syllables in her name. I hope this pisses her off

"Sharon, that seems fair. Here take this bag, draw some and do your lab test. And, could you do me a favor, Sharon?"

"What is that, Bob."

"Sharon, would you tell your associates in the cars to lower their headlights. I like being a star, but would be more relaxed out of this particular spotlight. And would they please stuff their guns in their belts or under the seats. Elaine and I are unarmed, and we feel more comfortable dealing with peers."

"No problem, Bob. Gentlemen please cut your lights and put down your weapons. Boys love to play with their toys, don't they, Bob."

In ten seconds the running lights form a surreal arc around my car. Sharon and I walk to a midpoint between her $120K+ vehicle and my used car. I hand her the bag, and she heads to the sedan. She hands the bag in through the passenger window, and waits. The sentinel remains at the pickup. I pull Elaine close as if to embrace with affection. I just want to speak.

"Go over to Sharon and chum it up."

As she approaches her old friend, the protector steps to intercept.

"Where are you going?

"I want to talk to Sharon."

"It's OK. She's cool."

Sharon is the shot caller here.

I can't make out the man's face, but I know I've heard his voice. And I've seen the strange way he points with the fingers three, four and five of his right hand. Not his index finger. The doctor. Or, is he a dealer, who plays a doctor when necessary. Is he a dealing doctor or a doctoring dealer? How real was

Maggie's examination? How much danger is she in? This is not good. The ladies are chatting beside the car. Sharon retrieves the bag and the two of them return to me. Elaine takes the bag and puts in the car.

"The stuff's not garbage, but it's not nearly what we were promised. It's about one-third pure. We were promised a higher quality. Very hard to move stuff like this on the street."

"First of all you were never promised a certain quality. Second, you were promised the stuff would be street ready. I have already tested it myself. Fifty-percent pure individual one-gram packets are street ready. Third, by now the junkies are jonesin' something fierce. They'll pay top dollar for this stuff. And the quantity will make all of them very happy. Maybe we should compare our testing equipment. Don't try to fuck us on the deal. Why not show us yours while we show you ours? It's what we have to sell, and you can't get any better. In fact you can't get any other. Yours is not a competitive bid. Take it or leave it."

"We'll take it for our price."

"And, what would that be, Sharon?"

"We'll give you 800 the lot, assuming you have twenty eight kees, Bob?"

"We have two weeks' worth of one-gram units. All you have to do is move them. No muss and no fuss. Just immediate profit. Plus, we have multiple kees, which have not been stepped on or repackaged. You can store these for sale later, break them down and move them now, or deal them off. For the entire lot we'll take the two million we mentioned and that you said you were going to acquire. So cut the crap and meet the price or we walk."

"You've got to be joking."

"When it comes to vast sums of money, I never joke."

"Two million? Are you using?"

"I do not use. And I am about to take the offer off the table."

"Are you threatening me?"

"A threat would be stupid and probably fatal. You have too many people, with two much fire power. We are just a couple of Uplanders who struck it rich and want to distribute the wealth. For two million you can move the load in about three weeks or less. Assuming you're a good businessperson, Sharon, you can make 20 a gram. I won't bore you with the math, but that, a big profiy for next to nothing. In any business that's a phenomenal ROI. But, if you would rather we sell to someone else or move the stuff through Detroit, we can oblige your wish. What's your answer, Sharon?"

"I have to make a call to my money."

From inside her jacket, she extracts a cell phone. Presses one number, whispers, then closes the appendage.

"I can do one million. That's our offer."

"To show you that we are reasonable, we will sell the lot to you for one million seven-fifty. Or should I call my other buyer."

Elaine cocks her head in my direction with a look of puzzlement.

"One million and there are no other buyers in this market. I am it, Bob."

"I didn't say I had a buyer in this market. I said I had another buyer. In less than eight hours I can be in Detroit and in another two sell this stuff for a minimum of one million seven-fifty. Maybe more. I am offering you this special sale price, because I was under the impression, Sharon, we had an arrangement. Obviously, I was mistaken. I accept your apology for wasting my time tonight. We'll be leaving now. We're off to Motown."

"Maybe I can go to a million two."

I remain silent for two tense minutes.

"Look in the interest of fair play, I'll agree to one million five for the entire lot."

"I have to check with my money."

"No. You had your chat. It's like buying a car. The salesperson gets one chat with his manager. If he asks for a second chat, the buyer walks."

The ferocity of my voice startles both women and the sentry by the truck.

"This is not like haggling over a used car. Either you cut the deal or there is no deal. If you use that phone to make another bullshit call, by the time you fold up the device and put it back inside your jacket, the stuff and I will be on the ramp at the second floor. So, if you want to queer the deal, make the call. If you want the deal, say so."

The hum of four high-powered V-8 engines muffles the street noise. Four metal bodies pulse, while four flesh bodies are frozen.

Another tense 120 seconds.

"I really have to talk to my money."

"Adios."

"Wait. I'll do it on Ellie's say so. But, I don't have all the money here."

"Let's see how that works. You claim to be sending for the money, but are really calling for the cavalry. After thirty minutes of waiting here, Elaine and I are fish in a barrel. Easy to shoot."

"Fuck, in thirty minutes I can be well on my way to Detroit. Sharon what do you say?"

"Let's do the deal."

"OK, Sharon, we'll do the deal . . . my way."

"What's that?"

"We will drive to a spot where your people can exchange cash for drugs with my people. You see, I figured you wouldn't have the money with you. So, I didn't bring the smack with me."

"I expected such. OK, lead and I'll follow."

"No. The three of us will ride in my car. Your people here can meet us at the appropriate time and place. Once you're in the car, you can use that fancy telephone to contact your people with the money and they can meet us where I tell them."

"Wait a minute. How do I know this is not a trap? Where you take our money and keep the smack."

"The place will be public, and you'll have more people than I do. You've got the gorillas in the sedan and pickup. Particularly mister doctor over there. They will be following us. Plus, you'll have the firepower of the people delivering the money. We're will be out numbered and out gunned. You could easily shoot Elaine and me."

"Aren't you afraid we'll jump you and take everything?"

"No, because, we have the element of location. We know where we will be meeting, and I'll have you very close to me. Plus, people in strategic spots to make a hostile take over, as it were, very expensive. It's like a stand-off or détente."

"Very gutsy, for a neophyte."

"Not a neophyte, Sharon. Did you see the news about the headless and handless Blacks found in Albuquerque?"

"Yes. They were part of a drug deal with Mexicans. A deal that went very bad."

"So that you know with whom you are dealing and how serious I consider this activity, I want you to know that I am responsible for the mutilation of the Blacks and the death of the four beaners."

"Yeah, right."

"Ask your buddy here."

"Ellie?"

"Bob's tellin' the truth. He smoked the wetbacks and cleaned up the mess they left so that we would not be traced. The heads and hands are in the trunk of a car at a rest stop on some Interstate in New Mexico."

"Damn, you are stone cold."

"No, dear heart, I'm just very serious about the deal, getting it done, and disappearing. So, tell your friends they are to sit tight while the three of us get in my car and leave. After about fifteen minutes, you will call them and tell them where they can meet us. This is just a big fucking precaution for both of us. You and the money, and I with the smack will make the swap within thirty minutes."

Sharon walks to the pickup, whispers to her partner, and returns. We get into the 'Stang and cautiously leave the garage. At the exit bar, I note a coupe parked across the street. Its engine is on, but not its lights. Sharon's safety net.

"Sharon, tell the *schmuck* in the coupe not to follow us. He can wait until the rest of your troops exit the garage."

We pull alongside the car. Sharon gets out and has a brief conversation with the driver of the coupe. We are off to the rendezvous spot. One block from the garage, I call Tim.

* *

"The Elves have left the building."
"Santa is concerned."
"The Elves have left the building."
"There are some strangers at the North Pole. Some boys who have not been good."
"Can you identify them? Are they cops or thugs?"
"What's the difference?"
"Not much I guess."
"The vans and their positions tell me they're cops."
"Then don't go to the house. Stay put for a few minutes. Talk to me."
"Don't go to the house. Stay put for now. Do not close down the voice box."
Walkie-talkie silence.
"Bob, who is that? Where are we going?"
"That is the man with the powder, Sharon. We're going to meet him."
"You can make it to the college faster if you cut down Lake Boulevard."
"We have time, Sharon. Don't we?"
"I don't know what you're talking about."
I slam the brakes and Sharon lunges toward the front seat. I grab her neck with my right hand and reach inside her blouse. Bingo. A tiny microphone hooked to her bra. I yank the metal button. It snaps from the fabric. She whimpers. I lower my window and toss the wire onto the street. Now I can talk without alerting the listeners. I speak to the two as if they were bitches that had just shat on a new carpet.
"Then I'll tell you both. Elaine told Sharon that we were going to meet her at the hospital garage and then go to a different location. Elaine even told her that we would be going to the main parking lot of the Hennipan Community College.

Some how, Elaine felt it was in her best interest to double-cross her partners so that she, Jaqa, and Sharon could get it all. And, then get it on. I'm really not interested in the why's of your actions, Sharon. Just realize I anticipated them. The bra mic confirmed my suspicions. By the way, Elaine, did Sharon give you the assurance that she would give you an equal cut of the cash or the smack for flipping on us? Asshole. What in the name of all that's holy could make you so fucking dumb to believe this dealer would be straight with you? How much did she promise?"

"She didn't promise anything, because I didn't tell her anything."

"Cut the shit. Don't lie to me anymore. I am now officially tired of your lies, and will not ignore them any longer. How stupid do you think I am? Did you go to her after you realized you and your lover girl weren't going to get the piggy share of the profits? Or, was she in on it from the beginning?"

The women sit in stunned silence.

"Sharon, what makes you think you can get away with this? I'll bet you're cop controlled. By now they know that I know. So, you're no longer useful to them."

Not a word from either one.

"OK, here's the deal. I am the only one with a gun. And if I don't get some answers in the next ten seconds, I'm going to inflict a great deal of pain on both of you."

The walkie-talkie crackles.

"Elf man, more bad boys have arrived. They are also waiting by the exit. What should I do?"

"Santa, leave and head for location three like we discussed. Now, damn it now."

"The bad boys will follow."

"OK. You can lose the bad boys on the streets and meet me at spot three. Drive like you're on ice and snow. Like when we stole old man Lockett's car. You lost him then. You lost the cops. You can lose the cops now. Do not go to the house. Is that clear?"

"Santa will meet the Elves at spot three."

I turn into a parking lot behind a strip mall, and stop next to a Dumpster.

"Sharon, close your eyes."

"What?"

"I said close your fucking eyes, now."

The report of the gun nearly deafens me. Silence is followed by a constant ring in the center of my head. The flash would have blinded me except I closed my eyes after targeting Elaine's left ear. The slug sprawls through her head and hits the window. Its force spent by the mass of bone and matter, the window does not break, but it is sprayed with blood, bone chips, and brain. Elaine slams against the door.

Opening my eyes, I see Sharon's mouth open and her head rocking. I can faintly hear her screaming. I exit the car and go around front to the passenger's side. Pull open the door and catch Elaine's body as it oozes out. Sharon continues her caterwauling. I hoist the female form to the left top of the Dumpster. Lift the right lid and roll the body into the garbage. Aptly placed. Close the passenger door and re-enter the car.

With the diminution of hearing, my voice echoes in my brain. I don't know if I am whispering, talking, or screaming. I look in the rear view mirror and speak.

"Sharon, you bitch, stop your whining. You and Elaine set me up. You must have known the consequences of a botched job. All I want are the profits from the sale. You didn't care what I wanted. All you wanted to do was save your ass. Do you understand what this means?"

With her mouth agape, she is sobbing and wagging her head. She waves her hands hysterically. She points to her ear. She is having trouble hearing me. No shit. She wants me to wait. No shit. Wait for what? She holds up her right hand and shows me that she is reaching in her pocket for a piece of paper and a pen. Frantically, she scribbles. Cops.

"Cops?"

I shrug as if to say . . . so what. More scribble.

"They got to me. I cooperate. I walk. No cooperate. Jail forever."

I wave my hand to encourage more.

"Know everything. The guys in garage. Cops. Doctor, cop. Roommate, cop. They knew when Ellie and I met. Never bothered to follow you. They knew where you were going. I had to tell. They kept me on a leash. Always looking over my shoulder. Now what?"

"You didn't have to tell, you chose to tell. Now I take control. Will the cops at the Community College follow my man?"

"Yes."

I beckon her into the bloodied front seat. She hurriedly scrambles onto her place like a lap dog currying favor. We proceed to the train station.

Terminal Exit

The back streets of every large city are the same. Narrow, dirty and in disrepair. The city fathers just don't care. The boulevards become avenues, become streets, become alleys, become open areas with railroad tracks between vacant buildings. Travel, whether by car or on foot, becomes increasingly slower and more uncomfortable. Train stations are located in or near the old center of the city. It's just that the cities have stretched and moved away from the stations. Spring rain is misting in sheets. Dirt has become slimy mud.

I have to decide whether it's better to park a block from the station or nearer for exiting purposes. I take a two-loop pass of the surroundings and spot no typical under cover vehicles, like vans. The cops are not waiting for us, but they will be here right after Tim arrives. I do see an Infinity Q45 and a pick-up truck on the same block. Each has a St. Louis County tag. Why would there be two vehicles from Duluth parked in this area at this time of night?

I know that Lexus from somewhere. The lights around the train station are dim. Is that because of age or the collection of dirt on the outer glass? Drain spouts are broken and hanging from the walls. Water spews haphazardly. The windows emit very little light. They are long overdue for a cleaning. The letters on the arch over the main door spell A-I-R-O-D-S-T-I-N. A testament to the deterioration of the building and signage. We drive down an extra bumpy alley that parallels Track 2 and look back two blocks to the entrance.

"We're going to go in there and discuss the smack with my associates."

"Both of us? Why me?"

"You are my insurance. If you are with me, you can't be against me."

"Won't the cops be along shortly? They'll follow your guy to the station."

"Hopefully not. As a teen, he had some practice avoiding adults and responsibilities. He can drive a car as well as anyone. And he is desperate. He'll drive through parking lots and on sidewalks to escape. By now he's lost them and they have no idea where he is going. He maybe late, but he will be here. We're going to meet him and then the five of us are going to leave."

"Five?"

"He has two females with him. And you are hereby invited to join our merry band. I can't leave you to face the cops. You'd take the entire load for this failed trap. They'd revoke your license to live. The cops can't let the feds or the public know they failed. And your usefulness will be over. You'll do at least 35 at Bimidji. There will be no *Get Out of Jail Free Card*. I can't do that to you. So to protect you, I can take you along or give you the Dumpster treatment like Elaine. I prefer to take you along. Your knowledge of the distribution system may prove valuable."

"Not much of a choice."

"True. Who do you know in Chicago and St. Louis who could take this much smack? Someone, who has the cash or easy access to it?"

She stares straight ahead and does not blink for a long time. With a deep sigh and shoulder's slumping, she is in.

"I know no one in St. Louis. But, I have two names in Chicago. An Ecuadorian and an Italian. They don't like each other, but their territories are mutually exclusive. We could deal half-and-half. Given the amount, it would be easier and faster than one buyer. The total take may not be as high as we want, but we can deal and be gone in less than a day. I'll need to give them both some notice."

"Good."

"If I introduce you to the two guys in Chicago, I am entitled to a slice of the pie?"

"Because I am benevolent, you're entitled to your fair share. It's like company profit sharing, only you don't have to wait seven years to be fully vested and fifteen to start collecting. Your fair share will be based on your performance. If we have to sell at a deep discount, you will have not done your job effectively. If we have to wait longer than a day, you will not have done your job effectively. These will reduce your share. Understand?"

"I'm not an idiot."

"But, you are feisty. And, as yet, not totally trustworthy."

"I'm apprehensive."

"That will keep you on your toes."

"Now what?"

"We go inside and wait for my . . . our associates."

* *

As we leave the car near Track 2, with the doors unlocked, I peer in 360 degrees. There is no movement on the streets. No shadows or silhouettes in the windows of buildings on either side. Rain has bathed the streets, but they remain filthy. Murky puddles have widened to be a hindrance to foot traffic. Stepping around the wet spots, we approach the main entrance. The doors to the right and left direct us to *Use the Main Door*. I see my reflection and am startled to see how bad I look.

I am drawn and my eyes are sunken. Hair is matted and greasy. Beard stubble makes me look ratty and old. My clothes are wrinkled. I sneak a sniff and deduce that not showering for two days and the excitement of this evening cause me to exude an odor most foul. All in all, the cat would have left me in the gutter and not dragged me into the kitchen.

"Where are your friends?"

"They may come from the shadows, or they may be late. We sit and wait."

The waiting room is three stories high. The walls, floors, and benches are testaments to the deco excess of the WPA. A mural above the track entrance could be a Moore or Benton, maybe, Dumuth. The farmers are harvesting grain. Reapers and tractors with flat bed wagons abound. Muscular men with chiseled faces wear coveralls and carry scythes. The sky had been blue, but inattentiveness has turned it a light brown. A train in the foreground appears ready to take the crop to market. Women in gingham dresses and children in clothes that mimic their parents' are happily involved in meal preparation or clean up. Everyone has a look of promise and strength.

The floor is brown-gray speckled marble with a strip of brass running between the slabs and around the benches. These look like oak or walnut. Each seats six and probably weighs five hundred pounds. They will never wear out or be broken by use. The lights hanging from the ceiling are encased in ornate wrought-iron framed milk glass. Above them is a huge skylight that covers nearly three-quarters of the waiting room.

Sharon finds a spot. I pace the parameter looking down every hall and into smaller waiting rooms. There are thirty-one other people in the entire building. The last train for Duluth will be leaving in ten minutes. Everybody, but Sharon and me, quick shuffles to Track 3. No one seems to wear leather soles and heels. Rubber is almost silent on the marble. Except for three-man cleaning crew and the two men standing next to parcel cage, we are alone. I sit beside her.

"Where is he?"

"Coming."

"How much longer must we wait?"

"As long as it takes. It is important to our future that he arrives and we execute the right exit. So we wait. And stop nagging. Tell me about you."

"Not very exciting. Rich bitch with lots of itches. Alienated from family. Screwed around with the family business. Federal investigators came down on the company. The board, my family, paid a huge fine and all was forgiven. But, no one forgave me. Went into nursing. Like the complexities of a big hospital. Always wanted more. Money, men, excitement. Always working on an angle.

Pretty easy to skim and sell script meds. Big time after one year. Gave me my lifestyle. Diversified into nose candy and smack. Moved in very, and I mean very, different circles from my hospital. When the heat came down, I chose freedom and became a worker for the cops. I helped in the recent sweep, but had to continue to serve the new masters. That's why I set you guys up. Ellie liked the idea of setting you up. She said it was over between you two. I have learned there are only a few differences between the big dealers and the DEA. One is clothing and another is out-of-office lifestyle. Both sets of men, and always men, are ruthless . . . they would kill to get the job done, and they are always on the make.

Somewhere in their twisted minds, they equate drugs to sex. If you do or sell drugs, you must want to fuck everybody. I'm in the business, but I'm not a user. I had to fight off the grubby hands of local, state, and federal guys. Obviously, since these guys are not users or sellers, they don't have a clue about the pharmacology of heavy drug use and the crushing effects it has on the libido. They also don't have a clue about business, which is always separate from personal. They just think every woman should fuck them, because they deserve it. Anyway, I'm here. You're here. They are nowhere. And, we're about to get out of Dodge before the sheriff finds out we left. What about you?"

She has had two major screw-ups in her life. I will not be the third.

"I'm just a shop keeper from up North, whose business was going under faster than the economy. I thought this was an easy way out. Strike, deal, and split. Two of the crew are dead. I learned a lot about all of them and me. It isn't over yet. I am going to make it. I will have a fresh start."

* *

The methodical activity of the clean-up crew is hypnotic. Two glide their big broom-mops up and down sides of the big room getting closer to the middle with each pass. The third empties the trash containers and picks up newspapers and magazines left by former station visitors. His pushcart is filling with refuse. The same jobs, at the same time, in the same place, for years and years. Mind crushing. No wonder postal is an adverb.

"Bric. Man, I'm glad to see you."

I was concentrating on ant-like activity and failed to notice Tim's entrance. Sharon gripped my arm. Will he ever learn?

"Where are Jaqa and Maggie?"

"In the car. Where's Ellie?"

"She's outside."

No, he'll never learn.

"How's Maggie doin'?"

"Not good. She started bleeding from the nose while we were in the parking lot. Then she stretched out on the back seat and has been stone still since. Jaqa is watching her. What do we do now? Where do we go?"

"We have to discuss our next steps as a group. So go get Jaqa, she'll want to input on this."

He heads outside.

* *

"When are you going to explain about your lady?"

"You mean the out-of-the-closet former lover. I'll explain at the appropriate time. I'll also explain your role in this Passion Play. So just sit and be quiet."

"Bob, or Bric, whatever your name is, the two guys by the package window have been eyeballing us for the last five minutes. I'm getting worried."

"They're here to pick up a package."

I sit and draw one of the .45's from the back of my belt. My hands inside my jacket pockets are filled. I stand. Sharon is showing fear.

"Bric, Jaqa says Maggie should not be disturbed. By the way, who is this woman?"

"Tim and Jaqa, this is Sharon, our contact in the big city. Sharon, meet Tim and Jaqa, valued members of the crew."

Smiles and nods all around. Tim places the two anodized cases on the bench beside Sharon.

"Now what?"

"Now we redeploy our force and head for Detroit. I have a contact, who will buy our merchandise at our price. Let's meet at the Midwest Hotel on Joe Lewis Boulevard. Is that clear?"

My voice is intentionally loud. I notice the two guys have left the parcel window and are moving toward us. The clean-up crew has stopped, and all three are looking at us. I hear a shuffling at the main entrance about two hundred feet from us.

"Sharon, duck under the bench, now."

As she slides away, I remove my hands from the jacket pockets. My first two shots are directed at the two guys, who were waiting. My next three cause the sweepers and the trash man to dive behind benches. Jaqa and Tim are in a state of real panic.

"Bric, no. No guns. Tony, don't shoot me. I'm with you."

Tim collapses away from me. His eyes are open wide and blood gushed from his mouth and nose. My shot struck his forehead dead center. Two shots from others hit his back. He was dead before he hit the floor. I grab Jaqa and push her under the bench. The five men are now firing at four men, who just entered the station. We are caught in a cross fire. Slugs are ricocheting off the benches and floor. The two groups of aggressive gunmen momentarily occupy each other almost forgetting why they are at the station. We're in no man's land. To make sure the confusion is complete, I get off three rounds in both directions. Now there is a third party to their firefight.

"Time to leave. Run, but stay as low as possible. Head for Track 2. Ready. Go."

Three more shots in both directions. Jaqa and Sharon are twenty feet closer to freedom. I'm five paces behind. As I run, shots from the two camps begin bouncing around my path. Incentive to run faster. I get off four more shots, to keep their heads down. I'm through the gateway to freedom.

"The smack. Asshole. You left the cases on the bench. Can you shoot, while I go back to get the stuff?"

"Sure. Go."

Jaqa heads back into the waiting room. My two shots hit the back of her head from about ten feet. The force propels her, arms flailing, face first onto the marble. Her half-headed body twitches as I get off two more rounds toward the groups. The empty gun is re-clipped with the spare. I slam the doors to the track and move two trashcans in the way. Shooting behind us is intense. The doors won't open until the guns are silent.

Sharon and I head down the platform. About one hundred yards beyond the end of the platform my 'Stang waits. The jog becomes a run, becomes a race, becomes a true life or death sprint. I grab Sharon's hand and pull. As long as I hold, she has to run at my side. We climb down the small ladder at the platform's end, just as the doors at the other end slide open. Two shots.

"Halt. Mr. Bricsonn. Stop where you are. There is no escape."

"Faster, Sharon, we're almost at the car. Run on the ties. There's the car ahead on the right. Go. Go. Go."

Olympic sprinters have nothing on criminals running for their lives. I have no idea what the world record for the 400-meter race is, but I'll bet we ran that distance in less than forty-five seconds. Leaping into the car, I gun the engine before Sharon is seated. We're away. To Interstate I-94 then I-90.

* *

"That was close."

"Close? Shit yes, we were in a cross fire. We could have been killed. Why did you shoot that guy, Tim? Why did you shoot Jaqa? What the hell are we going to Chicago for, since you left the smack at the train station? We have nothing to sell. Are we going to Chicago or Detroit? What about that woman, Maggie? You just left her for the cops."

"Shut the fuck up. After you catch your breath, I'll explain."

"OK, please explain now."

"Maggie is dead. She probably died on the trip from the parking lot to the station. Tim killed her a few days ago. Tim fucked up three times and was a real liability. Everything he touched turned to shit. The guy, Tony, whose name Tim called right before I shot him is a thug from Duluth. Tony Nuccio owns *Nooners* and washes mob money through the saloon. When we robbed the bank truck, we took his dirty laundry. Somehow Tim got to him right after the robbery. Tony has been paying Tim for some time, I suspect. That would explain Tim's ability to support gambling losses, buy drugs, and pay for hookers.

Tony wanted his money back or better yet, the drugs his money would buy. Tim wanted to be made right. So, he tipped off Tony's guys about our delivery date, and he steered us to the train station. Your friends, the cops, could have followed Tim with their eyes closed. So, Timmy boy leads himself into a big shoot 'em up. I just figured it all out before he did. Tim had to die.

Jaqa was an execution of moral indignation. She stole my lover. She left her husband. She was disruptively greedy. She turned. And, I didn't like her. So she went away. And, as for the smack. If you really think I would have entrusted the merchandise to Tim the screw up, you have much more to learn about me.

Resting in the spare tire well of the trunk are two anodized cases, exactly like the ones I left on the bench. The difference is that my two hold the fruits of my labor. Now, let's discuss you. I need you to introduce me to the buyers in Chicago. As stated before, if I can cut the deal fast for a big chunk of money, you will be rewarded handsomely. Then you have to make a decision. Either you go with me or go away."

"How do you mean go away? Go away like the others in your crew or just leave your sight?"

"Leave with me is also an option. You've done nothing to endanger me, so I have no reason to harm you. How would you like to go away? Cash in hand to a new life. Where would you like to go? Think of your options. You have until the deal to decide."

WINDY CITY MADNESS

I have a sense that there isn't an honest crook in the upper Midwest. I've been rejected more times than a five-foot-six inch shooting guard. Maybe Sharon will be my good luck charm. For both our sakes, I hope so. Interstate driving is boring. Interstate driving at night is mind numbing. But, it's fast. Most troopers are asleep. The ones that are on duty most likely seek the comfort of rest stops and their eateries. They can spring into action if any is needed. Meanwhile the road is the domain of truckers.

Road warriors in two-sectioned tanks that nearly fly over the concrete. They hunt at night and seek rest and nourishment at the rest stops during the day. Each cabin is larger and each box is more garishly decorated than the last. The cabins seem to be as tall as a two-story house. It takes a minimum of three steps to rise from the ground to the door entrance. I wonder if each has a kitchen and bathroom to complement the bedroom behind the large overstuffed bench seat. The logo design and the pithy marketing promise, each more outrageous than the last, look as if they are the work of the junior class at a local art school, or *Deadheads*. Rarely do these leviathans of the lanes travel in pairs. This makes the dissonance of design more disturbing.

She sleeps. My mind wanders through the last week. Since a silent recapitulation notes only those events, which the mind deems significant, I am intrigued by what my mind considers wheat and what, upon examination, is chaff.

Sawing of heads and hands. The dead bank guard. The partial structure in which we bought the heroin. The circle of animosity at the purchase. The mistrust everywhere. Maggie's battered body. Tim's drunkenness. USA Today. The table where we cut the drugs. Elaine's telephone calls to Sharon. Driving, incessant driving. The confusing similarity of the motels. The guns. Shooting people.

The images bounce around and mingle. My companion sleeps. I can't afford to sleep. We need to stop for coffee, a stretch, and for Sharon to call her associates. This time I'll stand beside the caller.

* *

"Is Rick there? This Sharon Fallon from Minneapolis. Yes, it's important. I know he'll want to talk to me. Please get him to the phone. What I have to say, I can only say to Rick. Yes, I'll wait."

She smiles at me. Ever so slightly the look of a seductress. She's attractive like a new car. Not sure what I'll have until I drive it. I know I look like shit. I'll remedy that when we get to Chicago.

"Rick. It's Sharon. Sorry to bother you at this late hour. Sharon Fallon. We met a while back when I came to Chicago. I was with Val Rose. We all went on a midnight cruise. Some bimbo fell overboard and you fished her out of the lake. I wore a dark green dress that you said had lost all of its buttons. Val told me to call you. He gave me your private number. I have some merchandise I know you would like. Very good quality. Because of our previous favorable relationships, I can let you have some kees cut and pre-packaged and several uncut kees. You buy. You move immediately. You get your profit in less than a week. Delivery tomorrow morning. You can sample. We do the deal. I get out of town. Where shall we meet? I'll be there whenever you want. Noon it is then. In advance, thanks."

Another call.

"Bert, please. Yes, disturb him; I have something important to tell him. This is Sharon Fallon from Minneapolis. I'm an associate of Val Rose. Bert, sweetie, this is Sharon, the friend of Val Rose. I danced with you at your daughter's birthday party. I wore a pink suit, which you said was too short for such an occasion. Thank you. Yes, Val is fine. He gave me your number.

I'll be brief. I have some merchandise, which I think might interest you. Good quality. Some cut and pre-packaged. Plus, some kees uncut and not packaged. You can buy it and move it in less than four days. Why? Because, Val and I have taken to the life of no-activity. Minneapolis is too hot. I'm sure you read the papers. Sure, call him and verify. When can we meet? Tomorrow at three? Where would you like me to meet you? Sure, I know the place. See you then. I know you won't be disappointed."

"They'll call Val to confirm I am who I say and that we met like I said. In case you're interested, Val is the last big time boss in the Twin Cities. He lets me alone and I pay him tribute. I'll get a good word, because Val will think he's going to get his cut. Only he won't. I guess that pretty much seals my fate. I'll leave with you. If I were dumb enough to stay here, I'd be brutalized in a week after Val figured he got stiffed. Are you fit to drive the rest of the way? Would you like me to spell you?"

"I'm OK for now. But, I will probably crash before the first meet. I'd like to be sharp. And a shower and shave would be nice."

"Yes they would. Maybe we should find a motel now. I could use real bed rest. A bloody front seat is not my idea of arboreal splendor. And, no offense, but you look like you could use the rest, too. We'll can set a wake up call for eight, eat breakfast and be at Rick's place by noon easily."

"I would like a drink before slumber."

* *

Before the next exit we see signs for the Pine Woods Motel and Pine Woods Restaurant. The bartender begrudgingly sells me a bottle of Usher's Whisky for fifty bucks. Ah, the benevolence of the roadside steward. I register for both of us. One room.

"Don't get any ideas, Bob."

"My ideas are about a shower, a shave, and a really stiff drink. But, to show you how much of a gentleman I am, I'll let you have the bathroom first, and your choice of bedside. Fair?"

"Fair."

"There is one catch."

"I knew it. There's always a catch."

"You did. Did you?"

"OK, what's the catch?"

"We are staying in the honeymoon suite. It was the only room with a double-sized king bed. The manager thought we would appreciate the extra room. He doesn't know how right he was. The bed size will give each of us space, yet proximity."

"Fair enough."

The room was testimony to the rural vision of a 1970's big city honeymoon suite. The huge bed and chair slipcovers were pink and lavender. The wood was white pine. The carpet was shag and there were mirrors all around. Three walls and the ceiling over the bed. The bathroom was fluorescent brilliant. The tubes ran around the vanity double mirror and above the tub. The tub could have held four. Maybe some other time. I crave cleanliness, the numb of alcohol, and deep sleep.

"Bob, I'm going to have to soak my pants for a few hours to get out the blood. My T-shirt is gone. I'll need to borrow one from you or buy one at the motel store."

"I'll give you a clean one. It'll be big, but serviceable."

"Now if you don't mind, I wish to remove the dirt and grime of today's activities."

"Can I pour you an adult beverage?"

"Sure lots of ice."

"I'll be back in a minute. The ice machine is down the hall."

The noise from the crickets and other night critters almost drowns out the noise of trucks passing on the Interstate. Almost. One ice bucket filled.

"Your libation is available. Do you want to come out here and get it or should I come in there and hand it to you personally."

"Very funny. Just leave it by the door. I'll get it."

Aliens 2 almost drowns out the water noise from the tub, the door opening and closing, and the splash back into the water. Almost. A long draft initially stings my mouth and throat. The second swallow slides right behind the first. One commercial break later and my eyelids are trying to meet. I never see the next set of commercials.

"It's all yours."

Groggy would be an understatement. Loopy is precise. I stagger to the bathroom, already hot and humid. The showerhead is in the center of the tub, which enjoys the remains of the recent bubble bath. Her wet jeans are drip drying from the showerhead. Why do women use tubs and showers as clothes' washers? I shed my filthy, smelly cloth layer and step beneath the water streams.

Cool water becomes, tepid, becomes warm, becomes hot, becomes warm, becomes tepid, becomes cool. I lather twice and shave. I may not be next to godliness, but I become next to human. A towel around my hips and drink in hand, I exit the rejuvenation chamber. Sharon is prone on the bed. Her empty glass is on the night table. My bag is open.

"I took the liberty of finding sleep wear in your bag. I hope you don't mind."

"I've got nothing to hide except the sex toys and porn mags. Hope you don't mind."

I grab a T-shirt and boxers, dress in the bathroom and return to find Sharon enveloped in the arms of Morpheus. Her delicate snores recall Ellie. My eyes close with the last slug of brown water.

* *

The friendly voice tells me the dining room is open until ten for breakfast. We're long gone by then. The future is out there.

"How do I get to Rick's place? And who is Rick?"

"Ricardo Martinez runs the South Side. He runs the entire game out of his very large restaurant. The restaurant is flanked by his department store and his bodega. The three buildings are centrally located in his real estate world. He owns an island of crime and corruption. He is the king. His power base derives from illegals.

He imports them. They owe their lives to him. They work for him and prosper in his empire. The man is absolutely ruthless. The stories of his sadistic brutality are mind-boggling. Rumor has it that he found out a hooker was holding out on him and sending money back to Ecuador. In front of her mother and two children, she confessed to what she did. On the spot, he slit her son's throat and turned out her eleven year-old daughter. Six underlings had the girl on a dining table. The woman toed the line thereafter."

"A real sweetheart. How do we handle the sale?"

"No Bric's Hardware. We'll be searched. I'll introduce you as a friend of Val and my traveling companion. Rick will appreciate that, since he probably thinks I'm gay. We take one case with us. It must be filled with a share equal to one-half the cut pre-packaged and one half the uncut bulk smack. Let me do the deal. By the time we arrive he will have confirmed my appropriateness with Val. He knows me, or thinks he does. Given your time objective, I may have to settle for 50 a kee. That will be the base line. Hopefully we can get more for the total package. But, and I can't stress this enough, let me do the talking. You carry the case and stand on the sideline. And, for God's sake, no rapid moves. The guys to your right and left will be armed. Do you understand?"

"Yes. What about Bert?"

"Later, after the deal with Rick. I don't want to confuse you. I'm going to nap for a while. Follow 94 passed Gary. Head toward the city. Look for Evergreen Park. When you see the first sign for Evergreen Park, wake me. I'll lead us in from there. By the way, thanks for the drink and respecting my privacy last night. You are a gentleman. A rarity today."

I know nothing. I'm driving to a strange city, with a stranger to do a drug deal with a band of illegals, who would think nothing of killing me. What the fuck is wrong with this picture? She sleeps. Road noise is my buddy.

* *

"Sharon. Evergreen Park Exit 12 miles. Time to rise and become the path finder."

"What time is it?"

"10:30"

"We have lots of time. We want to be prompt, but not early. To Rick we should be there no later than ten minutes. He'll keep us waiting for twenty more to make sure we know who's the boss. We have time for coffee. A little cup of high-energy juice and some bread with molasses. I know a place near his restaurant where we can sit outside and be seen. Those who see us will let him know we are in the neighborhood, but honoring his timeframe. Deference to his position. At the bottom of the exit ramp, take a left and go six lights. Then make a right and go six more lights. At that point we are on his island. So we must drive as if we belong. Not like outsiders. OK."

"Si, heffe."

"The Skandahoovian knows the language. How quaint."

"Six lights and left. Six and home."

"See that café on the corner of the next block. That's where we'll want to be seen sipping coffee. Park anywhere. No one ever gets tickets in this neighborhood."

I pull in near a fire hydrant. We exit leaving the cases in the car. That makes me nervous. As Sharon leads me to *Café Quito*, I notice there are more eyes on us that on the President during a golf outing. Except these eyes are there for the protection of their territory not us. Sharon orders for us. I pay.

"Be slow and casual, as if you have been here many times before. Smile when smiled at, but don't invite conversation. Now what would you like to talk about?"

"About getting out of here with my skin intact. No puncture holes."

"Relax. Rick told his eyes and ears to expect us. We are just fulfilling his prophecy. In twenty minutes, we will get up and head back to the car. You will remove one case from the trunk. Make sure everybody sees you remove only a case. No tricks. They're very suspicious. Then we will walk down the block to the large building on the right side. That will be his restaurant. Then I do all the rest. You follow. How do you like the coffee?"

"Syrupy and bitter. I'm always willing to go native to appease the locals. The toast is really good. I was hungry."

"Shall we set upon our appointed rounds?"

I do as I am told. We stop at the door to the restaurant. Sharon knocks.

"Deliveries in back."

"No delivery. I'm here to see Senor Martinez."

"No here. Come back tonight."

"No come back tonight. See Senor Martinez now or you are in deep caca. Tell him Senorita Sharon is here. Comprende?"

"You wait."

Five minutes and the door opens a crack.

"Senor Martinez is not here. But, he will be here around ten tonight. Come back then."

"Listen carefully. I'm only going to say this once. I am Sharon Fallon. I have an appointment with Rick Martinez. We have some business to conduct. If you don't let me see him now, I will tell him later tonight that some asshole in a green pullover, matching pants and a fat belly queered his chance to make a half a million dollars. So, since I know he is there, the choice is yours to make. Let me in and live or keep me out and die."

The door opens enough for the two of us to squeeze into the dark cave. We stop two paces inside and the door is closed. The thud has an eerie finality. Sharon is patted down. I hand the case to her and I receive the same treatment. As she is returning the case, a hand grabs the handle.

"Get your mother fucking greasy paw off Rick's merchandise now."

Sharon is in control for now.

We are led passed the maitre d's station to the rear of the first floor. Up a staircase to the balcony section. Reserved for dignitaries and family. We are ushered to the center table and chairs are pulled away for us to sit. We wait surrounded by a half dozen stone-faced *plumans*. Or are they *huants*? Did they buy their green outfits at the same store as the Mexicans? We wait in silence.

"Miss Sharon, it's so nice to see you."

Rick approaches from the darkness and we rise. He kisses Sharon's hand. The three of us sit. Rick's back is closest to a wall with no doors.

"And who is your friend?"

"Rick, this is Bob Welch. He is one of my new associates."

"New associates? Val did not mention him to me."

"Most likely slipped his mind. Shall we get down to the business at hand?"

"Always in a hurry. Sharon, you must slow down and enjoy life. Would you like some food or a drink while we work?"

"Always the gracious host, Rick. I'm sorry, but we have to return to Minneapolis immediately upon the conclusion of our transaction. But, I will be returning to Chicago soon on a personal matter. Then, we can dine, if that is acceptable to you?"

"Yes, indeed. May I see what you have to offer?"

I hand the case to Rick. He does not touch it. A *huant* comes from the darkness and removes the case from in front of Rick. The clicks tell me it's open. Immediately the *huant* returns the open case. Rick removes the full bag and hands it to the *huant*. I assume for testing.

"Rick, your associate will determine that the contents of the kee bag are ninety-percent pure. The remaining bags contain one-gram packets and are street ready at fifty-percent. They can be on the street this afternoon. You can earn your total profit in less than a week. That's faster turn around than you're used to. Plus, there are two other kees uncut. Val and I feel this merchandise is worth 60 per kee to you. Nine hundred thousand for the lot."

Another *pluman* leans into Rick's ear. The boss smiles like a barracuda.

"Miss Sharon, because of our long-standing and fruitful relationship with Val Rose, I am prepared to buy the total amount in the case for 600 thousand."

"Senor Martinez, in the spirit of compromise, Val and I will sell the quantity in the case to a well-respected business friend for 750 thousand."

The two predators stare at each other, never once blinking but smiling like Barracudas for two minutes.

"Good. Done."

He snaps his fingers and a third *huant* places a very expensive leather attaché case in front of Sharon. She slides it to me. I am about to open and count, when her hand slams down on the top.

"Bob, to count the money would mean that you don't trust Senor Martinez. If you do not trust him, you disrespect him. That is not our way. Senor, please forgive Bob. He is new to our ways. He is used to dealing with the crude animals of the North. Those with no trust and no respect. I apologize for his actions."

"Sir, I apologize. I meant no disrespect. Please forgive my actions."

"You are forgiven. This time."

"Rick, we must be on our way. Do not think this an insult. It is a matter of expediency. I'll let you know a few days before my return. We shall enjoy an evening together then."

Our chairs are pulled away and we are escorted to the door. Two men walk us to our car and we drive to our second appointment.

* *

"Next stop, River Grove. Get back on Interstate 90 West. We have to go through downtown on the Interstate or drive through the city streets. The latter is shorter, but longer. The trip should take a little amore than an hour, which will put us at the warehouse on time."

"Who is Bert?"

"Alberto Dolomacosico. He runs a restaurant supply business. Half of the restaurants in the whole city buy from his organization. Many because they have to or lose the fronts of their buildings. The fleet of trucks and constant deliveries give him the network to distribute drugs and enforce his code of law. That's not totally fair. Bert is almost retired. Or, as close to retirement as his profession will permit. Regardless. His three sons run *Mama's Kitchen*. And they run the day-to-day of the real enterprise. The operation is 100% Italian.

From warehouse janitor to bookkeeper, from driver to Bert, everyone is Italian. And very, very loyal. They are good soldiers. If someone from the outside gives a driver or any low-level employee a hard time, that person wakes up dead. Conversely, if an outsider bad mouths Bert or his sons, the outsider will find his business burned to the ground. Bert and his family have worked hard to protect their own, and they have kept the riff-raff out. They define riff-raff as non-Italian. Bert and his sons deal with Val, because we are fair suppliers and we honor Bert's territory. Once again, be cool. No guns, and speak only when spoken to."

"Yes mommy. Listen, I have two tickets to Dallas. American. We leave at 6:35 tonight. Once we arrive, we have choices. I was thinking a farm near Brownsville. We can get reintroduced to society, pay someone to work the farm, and get to the beach in less than an hour. Waddaya' think?"

"Not my style. My style is more like Dallas or Houston. High-rise. Nightclubs. The fine arts. Twentieth century adult not nineteenth century dirt farmer. I can't scale back my life just because you think it would be quaint."

"Fair enough. We'll split in Dallas."

"Split the money, too?"

"Yes, fifty-fifty."

"Thanks."

Sharon slips her hand between my thighs and nibbles my ear. Is this a kiss good-by or an invitation? Then I see it. The triple serpentine of slow moving metal.

"Road repair leads to road rage. I don't do well with delays. Particularly now. If we're late for your friend, Bert, we may miss our flight."

"Relax. I can see the DOT signs warning of construction delays. We'll be passed this mess in twenty minutes. Still have enough time to close the deal and get to O'Hare. It'll will just be tight, because we'll have to come back this way."

"Fucking DOT. If they make us miss our flight, what will we do?"

"We'll cancel this flight and get another. It's not like we need to save money."

"Damn, I've planned so well, I hate to see this thing come unraveled at the last moment."

"Just chill. We're fine for time."

We are through the bottleneck in twenty-five minutes, and I start to look for River Grove signs. 2:40 on the car clock. 2:38 on my wristwatch. I figure an hour for the deal and two hours with this traffic jam at rush hour to get to the airport. It'll be close.

"How much farther?"

"Twenty minutes. Maybe a little more. There's the sign. Six miles. When you get to the bottom of the exit ramp, take a right and go three traffic lights. At the third light take a left and the first right. It will be an alley that goes behind the warehouse."

Another big city old neighborhood, juts like the one we left. Two things puzzle me. She claims a slight acquaintance of these two men. So slight, they need a reference about her from this guy Val. Yet, she has detailed knowledge of their histories, operations, and the whereabouts of their keeps. Second, I've seen floral delivery vans . . . the same ones near Rick's and now near Bert's. Rarely do florists deliver all over a large area like Chicago. Jesus! Am I paranoid?

* *

"Just like before. Follow my lead. Now get the case."

We park the car in a *visitor* spot, beyond the trucks unloading factory merchandise and the vans being filled with orders. No one pays any attention to us. No one except the person who is monitoring the surveillance cameras. As we climb the steps to the dock, we are greeted by a man in his mid to late thirties. He has so much gold on his fingers, wrists, and neck he's not allowed outside during a lightening storm.

"Can I help you?"

"Yes, we're here to see Mr. Alberto Dolomacosico."

"He's not here."

"Sir, if you would be so kind. Please tell your boss that Sharon Fallon is here. I am sorry we are late, but construction on the Interstate held us up. I know Mr. Dolomacosico will want to see what we have brought him."

"Give it to me and I'll decide."

"I'd gladly let you have the case. But, then I would have to explain to Mr. Dolomacosico that you interfered with the business transaction he and I were to have. My guess is that would make him cranky. But, it's your choice."

"Wait here. He might be in his office. I'll see."

Sharon winks at me. Now all human eyes are on us. The loading activity has stopped, the unloading continues. The young man is accompanied by an older, distinguished gentleman. The older man walks slowly and with a limp.

"Ms. Fallon. It's nice to see you. How have you been? How is Val?"

He kisses her on the cheeks. Very deferential.

"I am well and Val is as cranky as ever, but you know that. The Leopard cannot change his spots."

"And, who is this gentleman?"

"This is Bob Welch. He is a new associate of Val's. I am trying to introduce him to our dearest friends. The associates for whom we have the deepest respect. Val is expanding."

"Mr. Welch. If you work with Sharon, you must feel honored. Welcome to our humble business."

"Thank you, Sir. It is an honor to meet you."

I extend my hand and wait for him to extend his hand. He does not.

"We are on a tight schedule to get back to Minneapolis. Val keeps me on a short leash. Bert, if I may, you know how I rush. I am sorry to set the timetable, but if we could conduct our business."

"By all means. Follow me inside. We can conduct the business on this floor."

The old man leads the way. We are flanked on all four sides by his bodyguards.

Bert walks to a meat and produce locker. One of his flunkies opens the door. Bert motions us to enter. He and the man we met on the dock, follow us. The door closes.

"Very safe in here. No sound. No cameras. Now, let me see what you have brought for me."

I hand the case to Sharon, and she hands it to the younger man. He withdraws a large bag, closes the case and leaves the locker. It's cold in here.

"Carlo will test the merchandise, while we agree on the price."

"Sir, you will find the merchandise is street ready. A few kees of fifty-percent pure in single-gram packages. These are street ready. Plus, we have several other kees, which have not been repackaged, and are uncut. For our favorite associate, we think a price of 60 per kee is fair. That's 800 for the total amount."

"If it is as you say, we will pay you 750 for the lot. No more."

"Val knew you would drive a high priced bargain. And he told me to accept what you considered a fair offer. I accept."

Carlo opens the door, approaches Bert, and whispers. Bert nods and motions Carlo to go back outside.

"Excuse me. My son needs to talk about something of great urgency. We will return in a minute or so."

The door slams and locks. Or did my fears hear the click.

"We wait and chill. Sorry, but I had to say that."

Surveying my surroundings, I am unnerved by the hanging meat. Leg quarters. Racks of ribs. On the shelves are salami of every shape and size. Slabs of proscuita. Cheeses . . . wheels, wedges, and balls. The interior is wood. Walls, shelves and the grated flooring are immaculate. It is cold. I can see my breath.

"Where the hell are these guys?"

"They're in control, so they're in no hurry. They have their money and our smack. We are in here. This is a lesson in patience. I know that Bert would do nothing to jeopardize his relationship with Val. He is too honorable. But, he is not above teaching us that he is the boss."

"That's comforting. Look at the time. We're up against it. If we don't get this damned thing done real soon, we'll miss our flight to Dallas."

The door is yanked open and in its place are two swarthy gold-chained men. It is difficult to make out faces because of the intense light behind them, but one is Carlo Dolomacosico.

"You must leave. Now."

"Not before we get our money or you return our merchandise."

"What money? What merchandise?"

I look at Sharon. She is not panicking. I am. But, I keep quiet. This is her party.

"Carlo, the bag your father gave you contained merchandise you were to have tested. Your father and I agreed to a price for the merchandise. 750 thousand. Where is your father?"

"He is not here."

"Bull shit. He would never leave in the middle of a deal. He would never insult Val Rose that way. Have you done something that would upset your father and now you're trying to cover your screw up? What have you done with your father?"

"No screw up. No deal. No merchandise."

"We are not leaving here until we talk to your father. Get him now."

As Carlo reaches to close the door, I spy our case on a counter about twenty feet behind him. Next to our case is a box marked *Mama's Kitchen*. The money? These guys are trying to pull a fast one without Bert knowing. In one frantic motion, I pull one gun from my jacket, grab Sharon's arm, and lunge for the locker door. Carlo and his friend are startled. Both grab the door to close it. My first shot hits Carlo in the right eye. He drops like a rock in a pond. My second and third shots smash into the chest of the other man. He bounces back into the area in front of the counter. As he twitches, thrashes, and gurgles, his blood is sprayed on the shelves and counters. We are through the door. I have both guns out. Sharon tugs my arm as she leans down.

"What the hell are you doing?"

"Since this is now your party, I want my own party favor."

She has pulled a snub nosed .32 from an ankle holster. We're off like *Butch* and *Sundance* in Bolivia. To the counter, and rip open the box. Money. Lots of money. My money.

"Where is everybody?"

"Who cares? We're outta' here."

"No it's not right that nobody is working the floor. No one is interested in the gunshots. Something is wrong."

On the loading dock we see what's wrong. About twenty men are standing and pacing around Bert. He is flat on his back and pale. Then we are spotted.

"Hey, what's going on? Where are you two going?"

"Avanti."

From the crowd of men, six shots are fired. The pops, ricochets, and breaking glass attest to the shooters' lack of accuracy. Suddenly Sharon staggers.

"I'm hit."

"Where?"

"Right shoulder."

"Can't stop. Won't leave you here. Take my hand. Only a few more steps."

More gunshots. These are targeted on my 'Stang. Four in the hood, three in the windshield and one in the passenger door. Open, jump and slam. We're safe for the moment. The engine bellows. Tires screech in reverse and forward as we shoot down the alley. One more step to freedom.

"Can you tell how badly you're hit?"

"I'm pretty sure it's just a flesh wound. I can move my arm. But, it's bleeding a lot."

"Sorry, but we can't stop for repairs. We'll do a quickie patch when we get to O'Hare. We gotta get out of town. Cops will be after us for sure. Our window of escape opportunity is closing."

ORD to DAL

Can't speed and attract the cops. Can't drive slowly and miss the flight. So, just like the Momma Bear, I'll do it just right.

"Well, what shall we do first, when we get to Dallas?"

"You mean after we have this tended to? Check into the Hotel Imperial, el Presidente suite. I'll call room service for food and drink. Then I'll need to go shopping. Clothes, make up . . . everything. The fittings will be awkward, with the bandage on my shoulder. You will accompany me. I want my clothes to please you as much as they do me. Besides you'll enjoy the attention as you sit and approve or disapprove. Needless-Markup pampers the payee more than the wearer. Fiscal seduction. You'll need a new wardrobe, too. Then, after an obscene meal of too many courses and too much expensive wine, we'll retire to our sky palace and consummate our new partnership."

Bonnie and Clyde. But, not in some cabin in the woods. In the best suite of the best hotel in a town that lives for excess. I made it. Sharon is not the partner with whom I started, but she is a mighty fine one. She has torn her T-shirt from the waist to the bottom of where her bra would be if she were wearing one. She made a few bandages and a tourniquet from the fabric. I could not help her with the struggle to wrap the wound.

"How's the bleeding?"

"Ruined my clothes, but I got it stopped. The bullet is not in my flesh. I'm spent and shaking from excitement. How do you feel?"

"Relieved that the ordeal is over. It seems like I've been trying to sell the heroin for weeks. Shit. Shit. Shit."

* *

The traffic slows down as we approach the roadwork from the other side a few hours after we met it. Instinctively, I check the clock. It's blinking. Some thing is amiss with the electrical system. I check the dash indicators. Alternator is fine, but the temperature gage reads red. Now were fucked. If we slow down for the roadwork the engine will overheat. If we stop for repairs, we'll never make it to the airport on time. No choice but to exit using a service lane. Push the car for twelve blocks beneath or along side the Interstate. Run the lights. Pass every car and truck. Re-enter the concrete ribbon after the work area.

"Nice bit of driving. Frightening, but nice. The pain in my shoulder was hardly noticeable because of my effort to maintain bladder control."

We pull into O'Hare long-term parking, and go to the trunk. We're late. Empty the box and wrap all the money in my clothes. Sharon removes her T-shirt. She is bra less. Her breasts are quite perky.

"How can I help?"

"Stop drooling. Wrap my arm after I put a few pads on the wound. I was right; the bullet just cut a gash in my arm. It's didn't stay with me."

We set about this battlefield repair with no one in sight. She gingerly removes her in-car bandages. She tears the T-shirt into strips. Clean bandages will not show the blood. The slice in her upper arm is dark brown. The bruise around it is the size of a playing card. It will be larger by tomorrow. Pads in place, it's time for me to wrap.

"Wrap around the bicep tightly to secure the two pads. Then wrap the big strip twice around to ensure no leakage."

I can't keep my eyes off her breasts as she stands in the daylight like a combat soldier receiving attention from a field medic. She is most appealing. My part done, Sharon takes a pullover from my bag. The sleeves are long enough to cover her arms down to her elbows.

Lock the bag. The clothes on our back, ten large in my pockets, and a bag full of money.

"Better leave the guns in the trunk. Airport security, you know."

I dump all three of mine. She hers from her ankle holster. I like the way she thinks ahead. At check in, we're told the flight will be delayed about forty-five minutes. This gives us ample time for a celebratory adult beverage . . . or two.

"Two MacCallam 25's and water. No ice. There is no time like the present to start living large."

I glance at the bar TV. Sharon wraps her good arm around my shoulder and nuzzles my neck and ear. Her tongue plays with my lobe.

This afternoon, Federal agents raided two establishments, which allegedly belonged to different criminal gangs. The agents claim that local king pins, Ricardo Martinez and Albert Dolomacosico, were arrested at their places of business. The DEA said that the raids were initiated, because they believed the two crime bosses had amassed substantial quantities of heroin, which was about to hit the streets. The DEA uncovered large amounts of the illegal drug at both the South Side establishment of Mr. Martinez and the North Side business of Mr. Dolomacosico. Attorneys for both alleged crime family leaders say their clients deny any knowledge of the drug. Agents believe they have shut down two separate empires with the arrests of the two bosses, numerous under-bosses, and assorted member of the crime families. More on this late breaking story will be available through the evening.

"Robert Charles Bricsonn, you are under arrest for the murders of Eleanor Rainier Martin, Jonteil Winters Williams, Thomas Zeigler Bowen, and Carlo Antonio. You are under arrest for wholesale interstate drug trafficking. You have the right to remain silent. You have the right to an attorney . . ."

Sharon's whisper, no longer inviting, is masked by the numbness of my brain. The baby-faced man to my left grabs my wrist and slaps a cuff on it. He then points with the middle, ring and pinky fingers of his right hand to Sharon on my right. She is standing away from the object of her faux seduction.

"Do something dumb and everybody at the bar will be picking your brains out of their drinks?"

"Mother pus bucket. Where did you get the gun? How did this happen?"

"It's simple. I have two legs and you're not very bright. We've been sitting on you from the beginning. Remember Jonteil Williams, Omar's wife and your wife's lover. She was a DEA field operative. I was her handler and her friend since college. In Duluth she was watching Tony Nuccio. He was bringing coke in from Canada and laundering money through *Nooners*. She discovered that your buddy Tom was on Tony's payroll. You guessed right on that one.

Ahmed from LA? His house and phones have been tapped for months, as part of a long-term investigation. So, we knew when his cousin contacted him and what Omar wanted. Our West Coast people followed Ahmed to Albuquerque. Remember the Mexicans you bought from, they were *Federales* working this sting with us. Mexican Feds, like Val and me. Both sides wanted to know where the smack went after it was shipped into New Mexico. The men you killed at the building site were good men. We knew where you stayed along the trail from the Southwest to the Minneapolis. Jonteil let us know and Tommy's calls to Tony confirmed it all.

The cops at the hospital garage and at the station were locals, who were supporting our efforts. Oh, and the man next to you at the bar is my boss, Senior Special Agent Valentine Rose. He has been after the Chicago heavies, Rick and Bert, for three years. All we needed was a fool like you. Some outsider who thought the system could be beaten. Some small time fool, who thought he could play with the big kids. Someone who was witless enough to telegraph where he was going and then leave a trail of bread crumbs . . . hell loaves of bread to be sure we didn't lose himm.

In effect we owe you a big *thank you*. Your stupidly heroic antics helped us close down the two largest families in Chicago, as well as the thug in Duluth. But, your antics caused a lot of people to die. For that, the last thing you'll remember lying on a gurney with a needle in your arm will be that we were with you every step of the way. You couldn't screw up. We wouldn't let you. All those loose ends and you never saw it unraveling. You are a fucking Amateur!"